THE ENGLISH PHOTOGRAPHER

Mónica Corcuera

Books

Translator: Jack Buckeridge
Editor: Aaron Devine
Managing Editor: Manuel Alemán
Designer: Ricardo Potes Correa

Published in the United States by CBH Books.
CBH Books is a division of Cambridge BrickHouse, Inc.

Cambridge BrickHouse, Inc.
60 Island Street
Lawrence, MA 01840
U.S.A.

Library of Congress Catalog Number: 2011938314
ISBN 978-1-59835-299-3
First Edition
Printed in the U.S.A.
10 9 8 7 6 5 4 3 2 1

I dedicate this book with all my love to:

Javier, Paulina and Mónica

———❦———

I thank my mother,
for having fostered in me the magic of and respect for
animals.

To my father,
who passed on to me the spirit
and determination to never give up.

And to Nenito, my grandmother,
for having made me feel very special and allowing me to
occupy a place of honour in her life.

———❦———

"To love life, inspires us to value and protect it,

but more than that, it ennobles us."

Table of contents

Prologue	13
Chapter One	23
Chapter Two	26
Chapter Three	33
Chapter Four	39
Chapter Five	43
Chapter Six	47
Chapter Seven	58
Chapter Eight	62
Chapter Nine	72
Chapter Ten	79
Chapter Eleven	83
Chapter Twelve	89
Chapter Thirteen	91
Chapter Fourteen	105
Chapter Fifteen	113
Chapter Sixteen	118
Chapter Seventeen	133
Chapter Eighteen	139

Chapter Nineteen   145
Chapter Twenty   151
Chapter Twenty-one   156
Chapter Twenty-two   161
Chapter Twenty-three   165
Chapter Twenty-four   171
Chapter Twenty-five   175
Chapter Twenty-six   179
Chapter Twenty-seven   185
Chapter Twenty-eight   190
Chapter Twenty-nine   194
Chapter Thirty   201
Chapter Thirty-one   209
Chapter Thirty-two   212
Chapter Thirty-three   219
Chapter Thirty-four   227
Chapter Thirty-five   233
Chapter Thirty-six   235
Chapter Thirty-seven   242
Chapter Thirty-eight   246
Chapter Thirty-nine   251
Chapter Forty   256

PROLOGUE

I emptied the glass of its amber liquid and tried to decide where such an extraordinary story should begin. The album with all the photos and notes lay on the table before me, and my two best friends, Catherine and Vince, were sitting like two statues on the other side, watching me as I opened the first pages of the trip that had changed my life forever.

For a few moments I remained silent, running my eyes over the first photographs that marked the beginning of that remarkable journey, puffing air out of my lungs, trying to get my rampant, suddenly erratic breathing under control, memories of Africa bloating me with air as the beating of my heart began to slow, as I landed back in the present.

I had travelled through Tanzania, in the east of Africa, where the mighty savanna seemingly grows in stature between skies and plains teeming with wildlife, where landscapes of natural wealth and trees of horizontal foliage, give the sensation of life in all its inexhaustible extension. And in that paradise, in contrast with the most beautiful sunrises and spectacular sunsets imaginable, I would discover its dark side, the other face of the world. In the north of that vast African territory, and on a photographic expedition, I went through the deepest and most intense experiences possible and stayed on for a time, trying to get over a pain that I could never have imagined could possibly exist.

My name is Jonathan Carmichael, a man reborn. I say that because, for so many years, I didn't know who I was. Or at least, that was what I supposed in the precarious perception I had of life and of myself. Now I know that I wasted precious moments, through my selfishness, through a poorly understood self-centeredness, which only made me lose my way and invest time in my personal development, in the recognition and success that I had longed for since I was a child. An ambition I must say, made more intense, because my father had left my mother, my sister Gwyneth and me, a short time before my sixth birthday.

I remember little of those years, but I do know that Gwyn and I lived in fear, listening to those interminable and anguished nights when battles raged in my parents' bedroom, as my mother cried and begged my father to let us go and live in the Vale of Glamorgan, in Wales, where she had inherited from my grandfather's sister, Aunt Felicia, a small house near one of the most fantastic crags on the Celtic sea coast. But despite her pleading, and in spite of seeing her destroyed, praying night after night before a crucifix that hung from an old sewing machine, upon which a candle was eternally lit, my father continued his tormented and incomprehensible fight, forcing us to stay there, imprisoned in an apartment in the suburbs of London.

For many years, I never knew what my father's real motive had been in making my mother suffer so much. It almost seemed as if he enjoyed offending her, to see her cry and be degraded in front of his eyes. The only thing that I understood then was that our mother wanted to give us a better life, far from the stifling tension, protected not only from him, but also from the dirty dealings that he had with strange people who visited him at home.

With the passing of the years, I found out that my father was involved in a murky affair of the government that constantly put the family at risk. And within his exasperated internal battle, which periodically he drowned with a bottle of alcohol, he discharged his anger against my mother or whipped my fragile child's body with his belt, roaring with fury that we were a nuisance in his life.

After one of those many rows, exactly a day before Christmas, while Gwyn and I were wrapping the presents that my mother had bought without my father's knowledge with the proceeds of her arduous sewing-machine work, we suddenly heard three screams, which thundered through the whole house. Seconds later, my father took his bag, and without looking back and without seeing our faces twisted by pain nor our impotent tears, he strode through the back door of the house. That's how I remember seeing my father for the last time, his back turned to me, starting his shiny Peugeot, the tires screeching on the ice-covered road, as he disappeared forever in the fog of the night.

With the passing of time, and in spite of the deep physical and emotional scars that my father's miserable nature had left, my mother packed our bags and took us to live in Aunt Felicia's house, where I had to learn to make a living from an early age, distributing morning newspapers in the town.

I had to grow up quickly, to become the man of the house, although inside I was still only a little boy hiding from fear, sadness and anger, who pretended to be strong, audacious and sure of himself. It was a mask of self-sufficiency that took my personality in so many unsuspected directions, save my emotions, which I kept tight under lock and key. For some reason that I still don't understand, my mother loved my father unconditionally, despite him having hurt her so cruelly. During the years that I remember, and after having established ourselves in Wales, my mother did nothing more than pray and work in the old rear shed of the house, where she had set a workshop upland, where she satisfied interminable requests for clothes, for which she received the few miserable pounds that barely sustained us. What I remember most about her was her infinite faith and her desperate fight to be heard. It seemed that her relationship with that Supreme Being who had robbed her of endless tears, was much greater than her own or any other suffering. But I, on the other hand, after seeing that her beseeching was in vain, fumed with anger from morning to night at God and his famous benevolence, blaming him constantly for not having given me a family like my friends had, or tiring of cursing him for not showing my mother's enormous suffering any pity. Finally, after not getting over the loss of my father, she almost stopped talking and three years later, was consumed by pancreatic cancer, and died, a little after I had turned nine years old.

I don't know what I would have done if Gwyn hadn't been there at my side, guiding me, helping me through the darkest moments of my short, painful existence. We'd been through so much together and now everything had been turned on its head. Life had to be more than just the two of us coping with one tragedy after the next. We'd been doing that all our lives. We needed something else; a new direction, a new deliverance, which came as most miracles do, when we least expected it.

Our maternal grandmother, Manny, lived in Kent, and after my mother's death, that was where we went to live. She was a remarkable woman and, never having lived with her before, we'd never got to know how exceptional she really was.

But we found out in the following months, when at night, before going to bed, she would play one record after another on her old stereo: the big bands, Glen Miller, Dean Martin, rock and roll, especially one called the Goldiggers, a swing classic that carried us all the way back to the forties. We'd sing and dance, doing turns on the noisy wooden floor, laughing and sweating until we'd collapse on one of the old living-room armchairs. It was an incredible introduction to a world that I had only imagined existed in my dreams.

And being introduced as we were to music and laughter, a host of other things seemed to follow suit. Gwyn, who is three years older than me, taught me board games that our father had taught her as a child, and we became deadly serious opponents over the chessboard, our favourite game of all.

Our grandmother also loved horses, her father having been a groom on the estate of a well-known family with connections to royalty. He taught her how to ride thoroughbreds, with the result that as a teenager she won the National Jumping Championship. All that stayed with her the rest of her life, and even at her advanced age she went to the Riding Club, Thursdays and Saturdays, and always came home with a broad smile on her face, no doubt caused by the flattery that the old club trainer, Mark, heaped on her while she was there.

She passed her passion for horses on to us, and we learnt to ride as kids, galloping alongside her, over the green hills of Kent.

On my tenth birthday she baked a beautiful chocolate cake, which I ate so quickly that it put me off chocolate for years to come, and would've ruined my birthday, if it wasn't for the present she gave me that day. I can still remember unwrapping the parcel with my eyes closed, with my sister somewhere behind me, giggling. And when I did finally peel all that blue paper with the little white stars off, I remember yelling at the top of my lungs as I put my hands around a small photographic camera, while I heard Manny and Gwyn clapping, as they saw tears of happiness streaming down my face.

"I love you Manny," I repeated over and over, as she sat down in her rocking chair and taught me how to load film into the camera, reading the instructions that would remain engraved in my mind forever.

I learnt to use it and dedicatedly saved every penny to buy and develop hundreds of rolls of film that are still stored in the attic of my flat. I spent all my time photographing my grandmother dancing, cooking and ironing; also Gwyn, and my friends, my toys, and of course Sam, my faithful Labrador. And in doing that, I used to think innocently, that if I kept the prints, I would always have those I loved by my side. But with the passing of time, and much to my disappointment, I began to realize that was only an illusion, although in some way, their essence remained with me.

That was how I kept Manny, more a mother than grandmother to me, doubly close, until that early spring day in '82, when she stopped smelling and admiring her beloved roses.

She left this world after a long and full life. But this time, instead of the sadness and enormous emptiness that I'd felt on the death of my mother, I held my head high, and my spirit remained intact. I worked my way through my mourning, until her memory became the very cement and mortar of my life.

When I was nineteen, I entered the University of Creative Arts in Kent. I'd decided to study design and photography, and it didn't take long for my photographic work to be recognized. I got a job as an exclusive photographer at annual events, as well as editing the university magazine which served as a jumping board to a professional career.

But regardless so much success at such a young age, I was still carrying feelings of anger and rejection from my childhood, which pushed me time and time again to avoid anything deep when it came to affairs with women. I didn't want anything to get in the way of the life I'd mapped out for myself, which was really an infallible defence against anyone getting too close, or having any sort of power over me at all.

And really, what was this love that I'd heard others talking about? It just seemed to me to be a physical and mental fantasy that put a sugar coating on the need for permanent sexual satisfaction. Love simply wasn't what others made it out to be. I thought that at the time.

But it confused me so much that I preferred not to think about it, which was the best way to avoid emotional problems and getting depressed.

I have to admit, however, that I put a lot of effort into my role of part-time lover. And I knew that I had what women were looking for. They seemed to pop up everywhere, and take me on, until I'd beat another hasty retreat.

At the time, one of those hot flings was with Jackie Guirmand, who gave me a Burmese cat called Morris, as a present for Christmas '86. It was exactly a year after Sam the Labrador had died, and while I'd never been keen on cats, from the moment I picked up that ball of soft, white fur, I was hooked. I just looked into those blue, almond-shaped, loner's eyes and knew I'd gained an inseparable friend.

Jackie was a medical assistant, who had beautiful green eyes and a perfect body, which had my wildest instincts on permanent overload, until one fateful day, she informed me that the contraceptive methods we'd been using hadn't worked, and that she was pregnant. I'd never realized until that very moment how serious the word pregnant can be.

The news just came out of the blue, and through a flush of fear and selfishness, I tried to convince her there and then to have an abortion, or if not that, to at least have the baby adopted out. There was no way I was going to take responsibility for any child at that stage of my life.

We argued for weeks, but she held firm, and with great pride and dignity, firmly decided on having the baby. The party was over and, depressed, I disappeared back into the night, determined to erase that chapter of my life, as soon as I could, throwing myself back into the old blur of unbearable emptiness.

As time passed, I knew that I'd changed. Insomnia came calling, and when I did get to sleep, nightmares were the norm. I knew I'd been a coward, and the face of my child frequented my sleeping moments. Night after night, I saw her as a little girl, crying as she chased after me, reminding me of my cowardice with every gesture of her sad little face. I realized pretty soon, after all of that began that hell has two faces: one reserved for the dead and one right here and now, for the guilty.

History, in effect, had repeated itself, as now it was my turn to abandon someone, as I had been abandoned in the past. Remorse kept stabbing my conscience. I looked everywhere for Jackie, but to my dismay, she had moved and left no trace of her whereabouts either at the University or with our mutual acquaintances. And if any of them did know something, no one said anything.

After a few years of searching, I gave up and devoted my time to work, travel and to losing myself in a series of new affairs. And in spite of so much individualism, materialism and ambition that dragged me through dark passions, I somehow managed to acquire close friends like Catherine Porter, who was and continues to be my soul mate, a second sister almost, who instead of judging me, shares and understands my life.

Later than the above events, Catherine married Vince Turman, who had been one of my friends from preparatory school. I had the pleasure of introducing them to each other at one of the parties at Radcliff High School. And they both continue to be a central part of my inner circle.

No other woman who passed through my life after Jackie could get me to the point of making a commitment. The fear of repeating what had happened with her cut most of those affairs short. As did the fear of love itself.

I had become a Don Juan in the art of seducing attractive women who happened to cross my path. But I have to confess that a great part of those words were a simple defence mechanism to hide the old pain and emotional damage that remained inextricably within me.

My life was full of contrasts and subtleties, and beyond my obvious selfishness, I was also deeply sensitive and artistically spiritual with anything that I trapped in my camera. A strange excitement would invade me in the dark room, where images would begin to form slowly and seductively on sheets of white paper, as they floated in acidic liquid.

CHAPTER
ONE

On one of those days when everything just seems to click, I came back to my flat after work and got a call from Peter Jones, an old friend and colleague of mine. Pete wasn't normally in the habit of ringing me up and making my day, but this call made up for all the rest when he invited me to go with him and Mike, another friend and photographer, on a photographic safari to the east of Africa. The trip was going to be funded by Geo World, an internationally renowned magazine and maker of television documentaries, whose primary focus was the protection and preservation of fauna. Pete argued that it was the chance of a lifetime, and would give my work exposure on a world level and boost my career like nothing else could. I didn't know what to say, but finally asked him incredulously, "Is this a joke, Pete?"

"No, Carmichael. It's no joke," he assured me, using my surname as he did when emphasizing something. "A few colleagues have seen your work and want to give you a chance to step up a level. In the beginning you won't make much, financially speaking that is, but if you show you're worth it, in the end they'll pay you what you want. We'll be off in a couple of weeks. Think it over and let me know as soon as possible. And if I were you, John, I wouldn't pass this up. Remember, you don't get offers like this every day of the week."

I thanked him, without gushing too much over the phone, and hung up. I was still working my way through the shock, toting the opportunity of a lifetime up against a host of doubts, not the least of which was being absent from my work for such a long time. The more I thought it through, the more confused I got. But in the end I was guided by my gut feel that tipped the scales in favour of me going. Besides, I told myself, I've wanted to climb Kilimanjaro since I was a kid, and stand on Africa's roof and experience what many had told me was like standing in heaven's antechamber.

Still, the mountain would have to wait, because according to Pete, our journey would take us through the extreme west of the black savanna.

I spoke with Maurice, my boss at Stratosphere, an independent agency specializing in publicity photography and after outlining my plans to him, he asked me to return as soon as possible for the launching of the annual magazine, "Photographic A," in which I had been a key contributor. I asked him for three weeks, detailing the noble cause for the safari, but he simply adjusted the glasses on his long nose, stared at me, and said "ten days tops," and wouldn't budge from that.

Everyone who worked at Stratosphere knew what Maurice was like, and there was no shortage of photographers around to keep meeting his demands. He was used to getting his own way, and judging by his reaction to my request, he obviously expected me to accept the time limit he'd set.

I'd worked eight long years at Stratosphere, and on many of my days there, had worked from sunrise to sunset. I hadn't had a holiday to speak of in years. And here he was stubbing out the chance of me having the trip of a lifetime. It was a key moment, and with my adrenalin surging, I resigned on the spot.

He seemed surprised, but no more so than me, and an hour after standing up and being counted, I felt an enormous relief coursing through my veins. I felt one stage of my life had come to an end, and this journey to Africa had appeared out of nowhere, to usher me into the next.

This was what life was all about, betting everything and putting it all on the line. And I couldn't count the days before the whole thing got under way.

I farewelled Catherine and Vince, who were going on a work assignment to Australia for a year, and Gwyn, who with her husband Mark, would look after Morris in my absence. The poor cat would have to do the best he could, and I knew that me not being around wasn't going to do him any good. In fact, the thought of me being abandoned by my father came to mind when I thought about leaving poor, old Morris behind.

CHAPTER
TWO

I was bound for Africa, but I had to get out of England first, and on the day of our departure, we spent several hours at Heathrow, filling out forms, standing at a counter, surrounded by enormous steel chests loaded with lenses, tripods, film and everything else that photographic work demands. Not to mention Mike's guitar, which I could already see him strumming under an African sunset.

A trip of more than four thousand miles, with a short stopover in Nairobi, saw us arrive in Dar as Salaam, the capital of Tanzania. The problem with our luggage that we'd had in London continued, as we had to wait hours at Julius Nyerere Airport, for all the disparate items of our equipment that hadn't been grouped together correctly in the first place.

In the end when everything was finally accounted for, and exhausted from waiting, we dragged the heavy trunks across the floor and out of the terminal, without any customs officer enquiring as to what all this equipment was for, or what our purpose in coming to Tanzania had been. And we were no better off, trying to get someone to help us, because no one seemed interested in our money.

We waited outside on the footpath disconsolately, until a "matutu;" an African taxi-van suddenly appeared. The driver nearly ran over a woman with a basket on her head, as he cut his way through the traffic and dozens of street vendors who began to yell, "Mzungus, mzungus," which we later found out meant us, white tourists.

Once the matutu had located us, we were surrounded by everyone else, trying to sell us their wares, as a couple of arrogant Arabs pushed their way through the throng, offering to change our pounds for Tanzanian shillings.

And as if that wasn't enough, when the van from the hotel arrived to collect us, the matutu driver insisted that we were his passengers, until logic finally prevailed and we loaded everything into the van and slumped into our seats.

"Sorry, misters," the van driver apologized, jumping in and closing the window. "These matutu drivers are a real problem." And without another word, we rushed into the traffic, past tall buildings and football fields, and alternating sights of poverty and wealth, until we got to The Hotel Uluguru, outside Nairobi, an attractive complex of buildings set not far from the chain of the most extraordinarily humid jungle mountains in Africa that run north to south for some sixty miles.

During the afternoon we would find out in more detail about the Gajha Gold Mine, property of the British company Goldstar, located twenty miles to the south of Lake Victoria, the second largest fresh water lake in the world as measured by surface area, and where catastrophic pollution had taken place and affected the economy and environment of the region.

Peter had told us a few days before that ecologists and conservationists from Tanzania and other neighboring countries had complained about the government's approval of projects, which had put the region's biodiversity at risk. And especially the gold mine, because an elevated level of sodium cyanide and other toxic materials, used in the gold extraction process, had seeped into the Lake Victoria drainage system.

We were going to lend support to this cause, exposing the situation internationally, and hopefully, as a consequence, put pressure on the government to protect this gigantic natural paradise from becoming a veritable graveyard for animals of every conceivable description.

The hotel manager told us that the Uluguru Mountains were home to thousands of species of reptiles, warthogs, and an astonishing variety of monkeys and antelope, among other animals. But what made it truly unique in the world was the proliferation of exotic birds, an avian paradise, visible from the balcony of our hotel room.

After having left all the equipment in a special room under lock and key and unpacking our bags in our room, we went down to the restaurant and met Mummbar Wamuyu, who on seeing us enter, exclaimed, "Karibu, karibu," which means welcome, in Swahili.

Mummbar was an ecologist who had been educated in Dar es Salaam, and later become a prestigious conservationist and activist in his country. He had devoted himself to the preservation of baboons that'd been under threat of extinction for years by poachers who primitively believe that baboon tongues possess miraculous substances that can cure malaria. The polluting of Lake Victoria and its tributaries, it seemed was just one more nail in the baboons' coffin.

The situation had created a crisis at a national level, and together with other ecologists from around the world, and organizations that were helping them, the funds had been found to create The Gambala Reserve, located forty miles from Shinyanga.

Mummbar filled us in on other problems connected with the gold mine. It seemed that not only was wildlife threatened, but the miners themselves had a very high rate of HIV, which had caused a problem for the communities of Mwanza and Mara, townships in the Lake Victoria district.

"However, AMREF," Mummbar said, referring to an African Medical Association that was trying to put the brakes on the spread of AIDS, and that had been collaborating with Mummbar and his colleagues, "hasn't been able to grasp the scale of involvement that we would like. Perhaps you, as representatives of such a prestigious magazine like Geo World, can be a great help. You could open the eyes of readers and television viewers everywhere, and put the hunters and miners in the public eye."

He invited us to spend a few days in the Reserve to appreciate, first hand, the crisis that was cutting through both animal and human populations in the region. We accepted, but decided to go first to the mine, which was little more than an hour and a half along the route to the Reserve. We already knew plenty about what was going on, but Mummbar had given us more details, and we were more determined now about what our next step should be.

After the long chat, we went out and had a look around the city, walking through picturesque open-air markets, where a cornucopia of handicrafts was on offer: ebony carvings, baskets, batiks and kangas, cotton handkerchiefs in bright colours used mainly by women, although it seemed everyone had some sort of use for them. I bought one and tied it around my neck as we continued walking among shrines, where dozens of witch doctors from different tribes sold natural remedies against an infinity of ailments.

After strolling through the market, we ate some typical Tanzanian food, a mix of shellfish and tropical fruit, and took photos of the alleys and their market stands, swathed in a multitude of colours.

The sun was burning us, and we were tired from the heat, so we headed back to the hotel, bearing in mind that we had to leave at seven in the morning for the small airport, twelve miles out of the capital, where we would take a light aircraft to Shinyanga.

Back at the hotel we sat on the terrace drinking beer and staring at the amazing sight of the mountains in the far distance. We got our maps out and traced our route through Africa in the weeks to come, but drew a dark, black ring around the Gajha Mine, where we knew the miners could pose a problem. The mine after all was their only source of income.

Still all that was in the future. Tonight was our first night in Africa, and we wanted to do something to celebrate that fact. So after asking around, we went to a well-known restaurant where a young woman in a green tunic, wearing a traditional turban tied around her head, showed us to a table near the dance floor. Two dozen black faces danced past our table to a Tanzanian group, whose beat and music sounded more Caribbean than African.

It was just what we'd been looking for, so we ordered drinks and stared at the hips of the women on the dance floor. They seemed to be in some sort of a trance brought on by the percussion of the bombo and a pair of rattles made from a hollow pumpkin, and an accordion that never stopped.

After a few drinks and a lot of talk about the exotic clothing swirling around the dance floor in front of us, Mike jumped up without warning, his hand in a girl's who'd apparently asked him to dance. We nearly killed ourselves laughing, as he tried to sway his hips and bend his arms like her. But while we continued watching his extraordinary impromptu performance, that now included him singing and dancing Bob Marley style, I asked Pete, "By the way, how's Sarah?"

He looked at me, thinking about Mike's wife, who was battling a serious heart condition. "She looks like she's getting worse every day. Mike doesn't talk much about it, but I know it depresses him. Her condition is very complicated. And the saddest thing of all is that he depends on her totally. I don't want to think about what'll happen when she's not around."

I couldn't think of anything to say. Mike had been carrying that burden for a long time, but despite the sadness, he always seemed to be the life of the party. He liked to play the guitar and sing until he dropped whenever we got together. But, as well as being musical, he was also religious, and maybe the mix of the two kept his spirit up.

After a few more songs, he came back to the table, his shirt covered in sweat. "Why don't you two get up and dance. We're in Tanzania, man!"

We laughed, watching him still on his feet, gyrating to the rhythm of the music. He lit a cigarette, and smiled back at a girl who walked past, then filled his glass with beer and drank it down in two gulps. "As far as I'm concerned I'd spend my whole life shakin' and rollin', man. Music turns me on."

"I can see that, brother. I've got to admit, you've

got what it takes. If Sarah could see you in action…" I said, shaking my head and laughing.

"Mmm…, if you saw her in action," he said raising his eyebrows and taking a drag of his cigarette. "She's got more life in her than I have."

I turned my head and saw Pete tapping his knife on the side of a bottle, proposing a toast. "The moment has arrived," he said raising his glass. "I want to share the best damn news I've ever received in my whole life."

Mike and I raised our glasses, dumbfounded.

"I'm going to be a father!" he proclaimed, with a quiver in his voice.

"You're joking?" I asked, leaning forward on the table. His wife, Claire, had been trying to get pregnant for almost seven years. "I'm happy for you, Pete. I can imagine what this means for the two of you."

"I can't believe it," Mike said. "I'm with you; it's the best news I've heard in a long while."

"Well, the cat's out now. Finally, Claire's going to be a mother," Pete said proudly. "And I won't have to wait that long either. She's already four months. I wake up every day and think that all the waiting's finally been worth it."

"Cheers!"

We clinked our glasses and gulped some more beer down, and whacked Pete on the back. And after a night of carousing, toasting, dancing and singing, somehow we got back to the hotel.

CHAPTER
THREE

The next morning, after battling what seemed like one squadron of mosquitoes after the next, which somehow had found their way through the protective netting, we woke up exhausted, stumbled down to the waiting van, and headed for the airport. During the drive there, we slumped against the van doors like three rag dolls, our heads rocking from side to side as we went. We were still yawning and half asleep when we arrived and found all our equipment piled in front of the cabin of the plane.

Mummbar had got there earlier, and had been going over the flight-path with the pilot, and from what I could gather, we were going to make a stopover in Ngorongoro, where we'd pick up a couple of vets, who'd fly with us to Gambala.

During the flight and after having finally woken up, I stared through the window at hundreds of wild animals running free across the vast savanna. It made me think how small we are beside the grandeur of nature. Africa, without any doubt, is the biggest paradise on Earth, and fascinated with what my eyes were now witnessing, I took my camera out and felt the old passion rising as I looked through the lens.

Mummbar noted the expression on my face and asked the pilot to fly lower, and get closer to the wildlife stretched out across the savanna below us.

It felt as if we were skimming the tops of the baobab trees as we closed in on herds of antelope and wildebeests that had been startled into a sprint by the sound of the motor overhead. The savanna was suddenly a great dust cloud, and beyond, in the distance, dozens of elephants plodded heavily forward, spraying mighty jets of sand in the air with their trunks, as zebras and buffalo looked skyward, petrified.

To be able to see all that close up was stunning, and made us completely forget the hangovers that we'd carried on board.

A few hours later we landed and collected the two vets. The first to come through the cabin door was Phillipe, a thick-set, red-haired forty-year-old, his hair tied in a pony-tail done up with a blue band, who started joking straight away with the pilot about the colourful, psychedelic outfit that he was wearing, asking him if he could get one of the same for his son. But it was the second passenger who attracted my attention, a blonde-haired woman with golden skin, whose long legs were bared as she climbed on board. She extended her hand, and in English with a nice French accent introduced herself as Marie. She smiled, showing a discreet dimple on her left cheek, and with a sigh, sat down on the seat next to mine, and began talking to Mummbar about some permits that she had apparently acquired the week before in Arusha.

I could feel my pulse racing as I listened to her talk and looked at her neck. The skirt was lower on her legs now, which was a relief, but the damage had already been done at the door. I turned away and saw Pete winking at me. I didn't wink back though, just looked through the window, and tried to get my lusty thoughts under control.

A short while later, the blue-eyed doctor asked me about the purpose of our visit, and calmer now than before, I told her we were going to make a documentary about the Gajha mine situation, as well as continuing our work in Gambala.

All the while we were talking, and in spite of him sitting two rows ahead, Phillipe didn't take his eyes of Marie for a second. It seemed he didn't fancy her talking to anyone, especially an Englishman in a light aircraft, a thousand feet above the African savanna.

I just ignored him and Marie and I hit it off from scratch, almost as if we'd known each other our whole lives.

She told me that she'd been based in Gambala for the last three years, and that Phillipe, her Belgian colleague, besides being a veterinarian, was also a specialist in primate infections. From what I gathered, she was from the south of France, but had lived the last nine years in Tanzania, in charge of the Papio Reserve, near the border with Zambia.

She was dedicated to the preservation of both baboons and chimpanzees. There was no doubt she was an intelligent woman who loved Africa and its people, and who, for that reason, had decided to live here for the rest of her life.

I was attracted to her enthusiasm and determination which made me congratulate her on having adapted to this strange, new and savage world that no doubt would have seen most others bolt straight back to the security of Europe.

She just laughed and said that her life was guided by her work, and that the needs to serve and achieve are what open doors and close others. She added that the rewards for following this star were immeasurable.

Time literally flew, and after an hour's flight, the pilot informed us we were about to land. I looked at Pete, who had been apparently taking a great interest in my progress with Marie. He formed a fist, and shook it at me, which made me smile but also wonder what deviate thoughts pass through the minds of married men.

Two four-wheel drive vehicles were waiting for us at the end of the landing strip. I said goodbye to Marie, shaking her hand, but reminding her that we would catch up with each other again in Gambala. I was glad that I got that in, as Phillipe took her by the arm and led her away to one of the vehicles.

Mummbar told us that we would be taken to a ranch close to Gajha, where we would stay the next few days, and upon our arrival, we would be met by two plain-clothes guards. He made it clear enough that we could have problems with UMAG (United Miners Association of Gajha), a group composed of agitators, corrupt officials and rebels, which had cut themselves off from the rest of the workers, creating a sort of out-of-control mafia within the structure of the union. Mummbar added, visibly worried, that we should only interact with those people chosen to meet us at the mine. Their names were written on a list he gave us.

I didn't bother to look at it. The situation he'd previewed was clear enough. But he went on to stress that we shouldn't mention Geo World's role during our visit. That would only create suspicion, he said, which would invariably lead to problems during our time there.

And he finished up by telling us to not say anything at all, because the bad faction would inevitably find out what we'd told the others. It made me wonder what we were going to talk about, European football?

But there was more, Mummbar said in a solemn voice. "They know that if the mine is closed it will unleash a catastrophe, but on the other hand, nobody there is doing anything to improve the situation. They don't take what we're telling them seriously. They don't even bother to divert toxic waste or undertake any structural changes at all. They just put up incoherent arguments, one contradicting the other. And on top of that they seem to be buying support in the right places." Mummbar paused. "The director of the mine, Kassim Mangandi is invulnerable; he's the nephew of President Cofy Mangandi. I don't need to say any more about that, do I? But as you can imagine, this situation isn't just limited to this company and this place. There are a stack of other gold mining companies out there, all trying to see who can make the most money in the shortest time possible."

He'd painted a very grim picture, and after the beautiful landscape we'd just flown over, and the magic hour I'd spent talking to Marie, I felt as if I'd landed in the middle of a hornet's nest. I looked back at the aeroplane.

Mummbar continued his dissertation. "UMAG will save its hide at any cost. So just do as I tell you. For all and sundry you're just a bunch of simple photographers on safari. If they find out otherwise, well…"

"Well what, Mummbar?" I asked angrily.

"They could wipe you off the face of the map," came his simple answer. "They're astute, unscrupulous people, who'll defend their interests at whatever cost. They're not like the rest of the people in my country. Tanzanians are dignified and respectful. Not like these individuals, who don't respect anything or anybody. The only things they're interested in are money, power and sex. That's the sad truth."

"Then why didn't you tell us all of this before? Why didn't you warn us from the very beginning?" Pete protested, with a look of disgust on his face.

"We were afraid you wouldn't help. Really, I'm sorry it's worked out this way, Peter. But it's important for my country that the world finds out what's going on here. Maybe one day you'll understand." He paused. "We've provided you with two armed escorts. They'll be with you all the time."

We were dumbfounded, caught in no man's land, not knowing whether to pull out or go on.

"So, that's what we're up against, eh?" Pete said sarcastically. "Thanks for the lies. After telling us all of this, I can see that the people round here are not as dignified and respectful as you were trying to make us believe."

"I didn't lie, Peter. I simply didn't give you all the facts," Mummbar replied. "I promise you, that if you just do as I say nothing will happen. And we'll finish with exactly what we want. It could be one of the best documentaries ever made. Remember you're supporting a great cause. You could become heroes to the rest of us."

"Heroes?" Mike whispered.

We looked at each other, dissatisfied, but knowing we had no option but to continue. We'd got this far and turning around now and scurrying back home like a bunch of cowards didn't stack up as a worthy alternative.

Mummbar seemed to pick up on that straight away, and stood before each one of us, shaking our hands, repeating his apologies and reiterating that soon the whole of Gambala would take us to its bosom.

We looked at each other with the strangest of smiles.

CHAPTER
FOUR

A few minutes later we pulled up beside another khaki four-wheel drive parked on the side of the road, and two men, dressed like simple villagers, got out, and walked over to us. They didn't look anything like bodyguards, but that's who they were. They introduced themselves as Thabo and Bantu. "Karibu, karibu," they said, greeting us. We returned the gesture.

Our driver got out, farewelled us, and told us that the supposed guides would drive us to where we would stay for the next few days.

During the drive, Bantu, as he was nicknamed, because he belonged to a Lake Victoria tribe whose dialect was Bantu, didn't stop talking. He insisted on advising us that we should stay together at all times and that we shouldn't engage in conversation with anyone, nor accept invitations of any type, or much less, attract attention by taking all our photographic equipment out.

He gave us, in effect, the same advice as Mummbar had done previously.

After a long drive through thorny scrub that scratched the windows constantly and during which flying insects crashed into the windscreen every few minutes, we arrived at the ranch where, past a perimeter of leafy trees, a country house with a large terrace looked out on Lake Victoria in the distance.

Bantu informed us that they had chosen the place for its proximity to Gajha, its privacy, and because here they could look after their "dear friends." Thabo, the silent one, and Bantu, the chatterbox, acted like the ranch's owners.

We took the trunks out again and helped the two men pile them in a room chosen for the purpose. Then they showed us to our room upstairs. There was a wooden bunk and a folding metal bed with some hard down mattresses, which I hoped wouldn't ruin my back.

Exhausted, I lay down on the bed and stared at a ceiling that seemed to have become moth-eaten over the years, closed my eyes, and tried to relax, desperate to clear my mind of Mummbar's revelations.

Pete and Mike left me to my thoughts, and went looking for the owner of the ranch. But a short while later there was a knock on the door, and a very tall, thin woman with a pleasant face, and lustrous hair, and carrying a bucket of water, stepped into the room. She explained in an almost incomprehensible mix of Swahili and English that she was Captain Mbongo's daughter and that the water was for the bath.

After having guessed half of what she was trying to tell me, I returned her smile and she disappeared back to wherever she'd come from.

I got up and carried the container over to the wash basin, washed my hands and threw water over my face. And feeling a little fresher, I stuck my head out the window and saw Mike standing outside, guitar in hand, speaking with Bantu, the guard, who was waving his hands in the air, trying to explain something that obviously I couldn't hear. Pete, a few yards farther away, seemed to be going over the details of our arrival with the owner.

With an empty stomach, I went down to the entrance hall, as Pete came back into the house, and told me that we were going to have lunch straight away.

We all went to the dining room, the owner, his wife, and Mike and Bantu, who seemed to have struck up a curious friendship.

During lunch, the owner, Captain Mbongo, as he is known, gave us more information about the mine, confirming what Mummbar had already said. But what he did tell us that was interesting, was that Africa had half of the world's known gold reserves, and that because of internal battles inside the miner's association and disputes between local miners and international mining companies, there had already been many murders underground in the tunnels.

"I don't want to say that the big mines are without fault, of course not," the captain said, spreading his hands out on the table. "Everything's undercover. And no one seems to be aware of what's going on. I think the big mining companies blame the local miners for their own mistakes. And doing that just adds to the chaos, and the pollution just keeps on rolling on. There are hundreds of children who have contracted strange illnesses around here."

It was the first time I'd heard any reference to strange illnesses and I was intrigued. But the captain changed the subject. "I don't know what you think of Mummbar, but I can tell you he's an honourable man, and if he's brought you here, it's because he can't find any other way to resolve this situation. He's always tried to help those in need."

"Something like an African Robin Hood?" Peter joked.

"That's one way of putting it," the captain responded dryly. "But he doesn't carry a sword through the streets. He's only got his word, and that's stronger than any weapon. I would even go as far as to say that many fear him. He's so determined, and many find his passion intimidating, especially in his presence."

I wasn't sure I agreed, but then again I was new here. Another month and maybe I'd see things differently.

"We know a born leader like him is what we need here in Africa. He always gets what he wants, well, almost always. But this problem's more complicated. There are a lot of interests involved. We've got to make UMAG and the government of Cofy Mangandi feel pressured by international opinion. That's why we're grateful you've come here. Through the magazine and television coverage, the truth will come to light," he lifted his cup of tea up and smiled at us. "We hope your presence here will help our cause."

CHAPTER
FIVE

We slept better at the Captain's ranch, the buzz of crickets a backdrop to our dreams most of the night. We woke up feeling as if we'd had a good night's sleep and after each of us had taken a long bath we went down to breakfast. The table set on the terrace offered us a postcard view of the impressive tea plantation and beyond. The rising sun over the depths of Urekewe, as Lake Victoria is known locally, reminding me that I'd just woken from one dream and walked downstairs into another.

"This is living," I said before sitting down, amazed by the scenery, and the banquet of fruit, bread and cereals on the table. As I took my first sip of boiling black tea, Mbongo appeared from behind a tree, walking towards us across the terrace.

"How'd you boys sleep?"

"Ten points, Captain. And thanks for the bit about *boys*," said fifty-year-old Mike.

"I don't think I've ever slept as well," Peter agreed. "This place is magic."

"I'm with you," I seconded Pete, before adding, "although, I'm still getting over the trip."

"You mean the nightclub, don't you, John?" Mike said. "I wasn't the only one who danced with those African ladies. And I saw your hand around their pretty little waists. I think you broke a few hearts back there."

"Don't remind me. My feet still hurt."

"Don't you mean your hands, Carmichael?" Pete said laughing.

While we talked about our adventure the night before, Mbongo sat down at the head of the table, and stared into the distance, as if he was meditating, before he said, "Did you know that in 1862 the first European to come here was a British explorer named John Speke?" We all shook our heads.

"It was he who named the lake Victoria, after the Queen. But it's had many names since time immemorial. Victoria's just the one you read on the map. I've often wondered if all the others who've looked out on these waters felt the same as I. That's something that one can never know. But I thank God that I was born here," I followed his gaze into the distance, and felt the sincerity of his words. "Did you also know that the great River Nile begins its journey here?"

"No, I didn't," Mike answered. "But I'm with you. This place is nirvana. My wife's always wanted to come to Tanzania. I hope one day I can bring her here."

"How about having a closer look at the lake?" I suggested to Mike and Pete.

"Careful!" Mbongo warned. "The shore of

Urekewe is classified as a high risk zone for malaria. You can't go there without taking precautions."

His comments steadied my enthusiasm. And made me think of the vaccinations we'd had before leaving London.

"At the least sign of catarrh," Mbongo advised, "you must advise me or Mummbar immediately. It may seem like nothing to you, but by hesitating to treat it, the consequences can be devastating." He shrugged his shoulders and sighed. "I don't want to be a spoilsport, but you can't just charge off here without knowing where you are going or what you're getting into. You can't swim in the lake, for example, because there's a microscopic worm there that digs into your body causing the terrible Bilharzia. It's a real nasty parasite and hell to get rid of, and causes terrible nausea to boot."

"So much for paradise," Mike said, frowning. "Anyone for a game of cards?"

I had to laugh but as I did I remembered why we were here. "We can still photograph nirvana, Mike!"

"That's the spirit," Mbongo said, smiling for the first time since he'd sat down. "You've got to be flexible in Africa, because things aren't like they used to be. The English settlers exploited the Urekewe basin. Forests were cut down and swamps drained to become tea, coffee and sugar plantations. We've got the best tea in Tanzania here, but we've lost a paradise in the process."

I could see that everything Mbongo said made sense. This was more of a briefing than a breakfast. And I felt a lot different than ten minutes before.

And he wasn't finished yet. "It's like my father

used to say: man transforms, deforms and extinguishes everything. We can only be grateful that there are still a few places left that remain untouched."

Peter looked at his watch and told us we'd better get moving. We had to be at the mine by eight o'clock. "Sorry, Captain. We can pick up where we left off later."

Mbongo nodded, and followed us to the vehicle that was loaded and ready to go at the front door. "Good luck, boys. And we'll have a typical Tanzanian dinner waiting for you when you get back," he said, smiling again. "Enjoy!"

CHAPTER
SIX

A few miles before Gajha, the landscape turned dusty, arid and the surviving scrub grey. It was like we'd landed on another planet, where an unknown colony of aliens had built a giant metallic and cement structure on the hostile surface. It would have been impossible to imagine a place like this existed in the middle of the African savanna, if it wasn't for the fact that it was right there in front of our eyes, staring us in the face.

A few guards stood in front of a grill of white bars, and one of them strutted up to the vehicle, as Pete hurriedly produced the sheet of paper with the names of the people that Mummbar had arranged for us to meet.

The guard ran his eye over the list, and nodded to one of the others to open the gate.

We crossed the metal grate and followed his directions towards Sector 1, leaving a terracotta trail of dust behind us, passing workers and miners dressed in beige and yellow uniforms in the distance, going about their business like white helmeted ants scattered across a moonscape.

When we got to the entry gate, an enormous, scar-faced black man barred the way. Intimidating and massive, he looked like a giant who'd just jumped out of a terror movie in time for our arrival.

"Follow me, they're expecting you," he said inexpressively, as we got out of the car.

We left the photographic equipment in the van as we'd been told to do, and left Thabo and Bantu behind to guard it, and followed the fearsome African along a passageway to a metal door. "Stay here," he told us. "Somebody will be here soon."

We watched him walk off and disappear around a corner. "I don't know about you, but that bloke and this place spook me," Mike confessed.

Pete and I chuckled nervously. I knew what he meant, but before I could agree with him, a young fair-haired lady with a face full of freckles opened the door. She apologized for keeping us waiting and asked us to follow her to the meeting room.

I wondered, as we were walking, how long she'd been working for Goldstar, because seeing her, reminded me with a jolt, where the money had come from to put everything we'd seen so far together.

The three men in the meeting room were in the middle of a heated discussion when we appeared at the door. But the expressions on their faces changed like weather in the tropics as they stood up to welcome us, smiling.

"I'm Roy McMahon," one of them said, "the mine director. And this is Henry Dormonth, the superintendent, and Mr. Galijha, our administrator."

We all shook hands and sat down in the seats offered to us.

"You're British, I gather," Pete said, breaking the ice.

McMahon looked at Dormonth. "Yes, and Mr. Galijha here is Tanzanian."

"Of course," Pete said, forgetting that he hadn't included Galijha in the question. "It's a pleasure to meet you."

I wasn't too sure who'd made Pete our spokesman, but he'd kicked the ball off, and had apparently decided it was better to keep dribbling. "We're interested in taking some photographs of the mine. We're doing a study of methodology and the process of gold extraction for an engineering magazine at Oxford University."

It was a bold start, brazen really, because I doubted that Pete knew anything at all about methodology. But he got by, in the next ten minutes, skillfully dodging questions and asking a few of his own.

McMahon seemed impressed. "Before anything else, I'd like to apologize on behalf of Kassim Mangandi, our boss. He couldn't be here today because he had to travel unexpectedly to a conference in Dodoma. I'm sure he would have liked to help you in any way he could have."

I felt relieved that Mangandi wasn't around, because I felt Pete had a better chance of manoeuvering around our two fellow Englishmen than a suspicious African.

"But I can tell you about our operation in Kassim's absence," McMahon said.

We all nodded.

"Basically, we look for the mineral, explode the quarry, extract it, and then after crushing, we grind it, and separate it by centrifugal force. It's treated with cyanide, filtered, gold precipitated, fused, refined and melted down into bars ready for sale. Every step is, of course, subject to quality control."

I imagined gold bars in a bank vault in some scene from one of those classic James Bond movies. I never realized all that had gone into their making.

"We've got the most modern infrastructure," McMahon continued proudly, "and are supported, by the most outstanding drilling companies in the world, with the most sophisticated equipment available."

The Tanzanian, Galijha, moved in his chair as McMahon looked at him. "And of course our worker's welfare, their safety and health are a priority."

Dormonth, a ruddy-cheeked, untidy individual edged into the briefing. "Of our one thousand three hundred employees, a hundred and twenty-five are supervisors, chemists, geologists and mining engineers. They're trained under strict rules, laid down by law. They're all committed to Gajha and the preservation of the surrounding eco-system."

I wondered on how many other occasions they'd repeated these same words, could almost imagine them memorizing everything from typed sheets of paper.

I looked at Pete and Mike, who were staring ahead, like two sphinxes, at the three men on the other side of the table. I felt like laughing, but suppressed the urge.

"Our methods of extraction are precise. After drilling one area, we detonate it," McMahon explained, pointing through the window at what seemed like a traffic jam of monster-sized trucks outside. "Then, using those hydraulic excavators you see over there, we load a hundred tons onto each of those babies."

Galijha coughed, interrupting the Englishman. "Tell them about the chemical process. I guess that's what they really want to know."

"Yes, of course," McMahon said, a little irritated at being interrupted. "The chemical substances that are used in the extraction of gold are basically sodium cyanide and mercury. But the cyanide solutions are very diluted, as well, their Ph must be alkaline. Therefore limestone is added to neutralize the highly toxic acids and gases."

"And how is the process carried out?" Peter asked.

McMahon looked at him, noting the pen in his hand, and smiled. "As soon as the ore has been crushed and ground, and after having gone through all the other steps I outlined before, the product is mixed in cyanide solutions for between six and seventy-two hours. After that, the residual is recycled or destroyed. And to avoid risks associated with the use of cyanide, we employ high-tech engineering, to avoid leaks that could affect the environment."

Dormonth backed him up. "We're absolutely committed to the correct supervision of all this, because our future here depends on it."

Both men looked at Galijha, as Dormonth continued. "We recognize the fact that the exploitation of the mine depends on the miners themselves. That's why our training is so intensive."

McMahon got up and walked over to a blackboard hanging on the wall, and pointing a long hairy finger, said, "Gajha has all the necessary funds to achieve all of our objectives."

Dormonth cut back in. "Our major problem is local miners. Or better said, clandestine mining carried out by local groups in areas close to the mine itself. They are unconcerned about everything that we have just told you."

A phone rang outside, and almost immediately, the secretary appeared at the door, and advised McMahon that he had a call. "Can't you see I'm busy," he said, reprimanding the woman.

"I'm sorry, sir. But it's urgent."

He frowned, left the blackboard and walked towards

the phone where he received the call. He was that angry that we all looked at each other startled. "Yes… Hello, Phil. What's going on?" There was a long silence before a quieter voice said, "Sorry, Kassim. I didn't recognize your voice. There's a lot of interference on the line."

Galijha chuckled then coughed. And when he'd stopped coughing, he got up, and excused himself and left the room.

"Yes, yes, Ok," McMahon said, before hanging up. "I'm sorry for the interruption. Maybe we should take the opportunity now, while we can, of inspecting the mine. I can't come with you personally, but there's someone outside who'll act as your guide."

We stood up, thanked him, and went to another section of the complex where we put on uniforms, helmets and boots. And on the way back to the van to pick up the camera equipment, Bantu came up to me mysteriously with a note he'd said someone had just given him. "The man said, 'don't let anyone see it,'" he whispered in my ear.

I put the note quickly in my pocket, helped the others with the equipment, and got into the truck that would take us to the mine. "You can only take photos in certain places," the driver said. "I'll let you know, when you can."

The plant itself was a mega-structure comprising cement towers, enormous warehouses, tanks and impressive tubular structures. There was scaffolding, pipes, valves, cylindrical pumps, condensers, water tanks and containers of every imaginable type. The whole complex spread over an area of thousands of square metres.

Our guide took us to the centre of the metal and cement metropolis, and we followed him through each stage, listening to his explanation as we went.

We took photos at will, without him saying anything, and arrived in front of the enormous walls that had been left exposed by the detonations. It was extraordinary to see the whole range of oxide colours from top to bottom, like some sort of modernist painting, evenly spaced down the rock face.

Before we continued on, and without anyone seeing me, I read the note quickly and surprised, passed it to Pete, giving him the same warning that Bantu had given me.

After the revelation of the cliffs, we went underground in an elevator that took us to a depth of 2,800 metres, where we found hundreds of miners engaged in a variety of activities.

It was surprising to see the size and quality of equipment so far beneath the surface. "It can get very hot down here," the guide said. "The temperature can reach 55 degrees Celsius during drilling operations, that's why we need those refrigeration tubes there. They come all the way from above."

We continued through the underground maze of tunnels listening to everything the guide told us.

"The rock from the dynamited areas is taken to a *hole,* where there are lock gates. The rubble is left there, until after falling through conduits, it is transported up to the surface in special lidded baskets, where it is moved to the plant for processing."

I was in an awesome subterranean world and, as I was standing there, trying to take it all in, Pete came up to me and whispered in my ear: "According to what this note says, we've got to get the guide to take us to the plant processor and from there to the treated water deposits."

I just nodded, and kept on taking photos, and after almost an hour of being shown around, we returned to the surface.

Peter asked the guide if we could see the area where the extraction of gold was carried out, which the guide agreed to without any objection.

So far, so good. I'd taken a lot of useful shots of the mine, and was starting to get the feeling that we'd get everything that we'd come for.

After a short walk, we arrived at the plant where the rock was stored and crushed, and from there, carried to a mill to be ground. At that point, the extraction process through chemical processing was initiated, the resulting purer solution then separated by electrolysis, dried and melted to obtain the valuable finished bars.

I looked at the guide, thinking what a unique experience it had been to walk around the complex, taking as many photos as I'd wanted. But I knew I was getting close to our first stumbling block and I was keen to test the water. "The whole tour's been really impressive," I said, "but we'd like to see where the residue and water leaves from here. There's a treatment plant somewhere here, isn't there?"

Judging by his reaction, I knew we were going to have a problem. He looked suddenly nervous, and began to stutter. "Yes, well. It's a bit late in the day to see that. Maybe if you come back tomorrow."

"No, don't worry about the time," Peter said. "We're not in any hurry."

"Well?" he shrugged his shoulders. "It'll have to be a very quick look. It's an area that's off limits to everyone, other than those employed here at the mine."

"Of course, a quick look's better than nothing," Mike said.

As we were being driven around, the driver, also our guide, picked up the phone and spoke in a dialect that I supposed even a Tanzanian would have found hard to understand. I had no idea what was going on.

The van was being driven faster than before, and the man was acting strangely.

When we arrived at the water treatment zone, the guide advised us not to take any photos, arguing that it would be dangerous to do so.

But when Mike put pressure on him, questioning the use of the word dangerous, he relented and said, "Very well then, but take what you want as quickly as you can."

When he wasn't talking to us, he was talking to someone on the phone, who didn't seem very pleased with us being where we were.

We knew we were in a prohibited zone, and took the guide's advice and got out quickly.

I walked towards a water pump, from where I could see two men in blue overalls in the distance, dragging something that seemed to be very heavy across the dusty ground. They eventually left it at the bottom of an enormous dark pile heap.

I moved closer, behind another pump, careful not to be seen by the men in front of me, or the guard behind, still arguing loudly on the phone.

And edging closer, I focused my camera on the lump that the two men had just dragged to the foot of the pile heap, and reeled back in horror, when I realized that it was a dead antelope. And that the pile mound was a funeral pyre of dead animals in varying states of decomposition. "Perfect!" I said to myself, taking one photo after the next, realizing that we'd found what we'd come in search of. I was so absorbed in my role as emissary for Geo World that I leant on a metal bar, which in turn fell onto a pump, making a thunderous noise as it crashed down, attracting the attention of the two workers.

I crouched down, and looking through a chink in the metal, I saw that one of the men was talking on a walkie-talkie, no doubt informing someone about the presence of an intruder, while the other man closed the lock gate behind them.

I dashed back to the others and told Pete that we should leave straight away. He had no idea why, but could see by the expression on my face that it was urgent.

The guide had just stopped talking on the phone and seemed pleased that we wanted to go. But when we got back to Sector 1, there were three men waiting there, including the giant with the scar who'd met us when we arrived. They didn't seem too pleased to see us. And we knew our welcome was over.

They told us to leave straight away, and that all visits to the mine had been cancelled for a month.

I figured we were lucky to get out of there in one piece, and as soon as we were underway, and past the mine gates, I told the others what I'd seen. I figured the cemetery of animals back there was only the tip of a very big iceberg.

"Stop, Thabo!" Pete yelled out, a few hundred metres down the road, as a man appeared, from behind some bushes, waving his arms. It was Galijha, the mysterious Tanzanian who'd been at the meeting.

"Did you get my message?" he asked, walking up to the vehicle, and looking back down the road nervously. And when we nodded, he asked again: "And? Did you find anything?"

I told him what I'd seen and this time it was his turn to nod. "I need to talk to you alone," he said. "I've got a lot more information that I think you'll find interesting. Let's meet at nine, at the kilometre nine sign on the track to the swamps. Don't forget to bring your equipment. You'll find it'll be worth it."

And without any more to do, he turned around and disappeared back into the bushes. We all had a lot of questions we wanted to ask him. But he was gone.

"I think this is all getting very interesting, boys," Mike said, rubbing his hands together. "It seems like you two had more of an idea about what was going on than me."

"There was no time to tell you back there," Pete explained, taking the note out of his pocket.

Mike read it in silence, and then we talked the whole thing through as we headed back to the ranch. Even Thabo, who hardly ever said anything, offered us some advice. "I'd be very careful if I were you. You can't trust anyone around here."

He suggested that we keep what had happened to ourselves, and to not forget that the prospect of quick money had made criminals out of men who had previously been good people.

CHAPTER
SEVEN

When we got back to the ranch, and after having unloaded the equipment, the captain invited us to the terrace, where his wife was waiting with the table already set.

Mbongo was interested to hear the details of our visit to the mine, and Pete gave him a rundown, but omitted the part about meeting Galijha later. It seemed clear that Peter feared Mbongo would be against the meeting. But Bantu had no such reservations. "I'm sorry, misters. But Captain Mbongo needs to know everything. He's the only one you can trust around here. What you plan on doing tonight is very risky," he said pointing at us.

Mbongo leaned forward on the table. "I understand your caution. But Mummbar has made me responsible for your welfare. That's why you're here in this house."

I felt relieved listening to his words and started

thinking of an alternative strategy for our meeting with Galijha, now that Mbongo was in on it.

But Mike got in first, interrupting the captain, and telling him about the note, which resulted in me finding the mass graveyard of dead animals. He said that as far as he was concerned, Galijha wanted to help, and could be trusted.

"I don't have the least doubt," Mbongo said, "that the mafia behind all of this is capable of doing anything. And I suggest you only believe half of what you hear tonight when you meet Galijha. Keep your ears wide open and your mouth shut. And discover through this man's actions whether he can be trusted or not."

It all sounded fair enough, and after almost everybody left the table, Mike decided to lighten the mood, by getting his guitar out. The black leather case was covered in stickers that he had collected on his many trips around the world. And just looking at it took us away from our immediate problems. He lit a cigarette and started tuning the strings, and while he was getting ready to sing one of his vast repertoire, I looked across the tea plantation at the warm African breeze rustling the leaves in the trees, while the sky above was a blend of burnt orange and red. As the first chords flowed through the dinning terrace, my thoughts drifted back a day, to the blue-eyed Frenchwoman on the plane.

The smile on my face must have given me away as I felt a pat on my back that brought me back from my meditative session. "And what would you be thinking about, young Carmichael?" Peter said. "It wouldn't be that Frenchwoman by any chance, would it?"

I laughed. "What are you, a mind reader?"

"Not really, but I can guess by the look in your face."

"Don't you think that sunset out there would make a man think of anything better than a beautiful woman?" I questioned.

"Indeed," Peter agreed. "And not think of all the effort that goes into building a relationship. The hard yards so to speak. I guess that's been your problem from the start, mate."

I didn't bother to answer him and didn't want to think about the hard yards either. The sunset wasn't about that. It was about yesterday, and Marie's long shapely legs and wonderful smile.

"Anyway…, what would we do without women?" Pete asked.

Good question, I thought.

As if the silence got to us both at the same time, we both looked in Mike's direction and realized that he was wiping what appeared to be tears from his eyes. Pete walked over to him and put his hand on his shoulder and asked him. "What's up, old mate?"

"I'm just sorry that Sarah's not here. I know what a trip here would do for her. It's always been her dream," he said, stopping to gulp some air, trying to get his sudden dip in thoughts under control.

"Don't give up, Mike. Sarah's a strong woman. Remember that the doctors can say what they like, but in the end it's God who decides. And you know that better than anyone. Just get your mind back on the present, mate. There's a lot to be done here. Just play the guitar and take in that magnificent sunset right behind us. It makes sense out of being alive."

Listening to what Pete had just said surprised me.

I hadn't realized that he was that sensitive. And I felt a stab of envy, at his ability to talk like that. It certainly helped Mike, who started to pick up. "Thanks, brother. You're nine years younger than me but you just sounded like my father."

"That's enough!" I snapped, slamming my cup down on the table like a hammer. And without saying another word I got up off the table and went down the hall, bumping into Thabo and Bantu who were talking at the foot of the stairs. They looked at me, but before they could say anything, I pushed past them and dragged myself up the stairs gripping onto the wooden banister, and slammed the bedroom door, leaving them all behind me wondering what had happened.

CHAPTER
EIGHT

I threw myself on the bed and turned the recorder on, and listened to the only tape I'd brought with me. I felt wild, and with the bitterness still in my mouth, I worked at getting my rage under control. I'd exploded, that was clear enough, but why? A great outpouring of anger had been triggered by something. And as I was still fuming now by the great river of lava that had surged through my veins, it took a time to cool down.

I put both hands on my face and closed my eyes and after a great battle with the inner demons that had created this insane outburst, I slowly got back to normal. Only to feel guilty and embarrassed for what I did. I felt like a complete fool. I'd treated them all, Peter, Thabo and Bantu, and especially Mike, badly.

I thought it through and I realized that the support that Peter had given Mike was the real reason for my reaction. It was exactly what I had missed all my life.

After almost two hours of dragging myself through

my own cobwebs, I heard the door click open and Pete poked his head around the corner. "Are you all right?"

It took me a while to answer: "I'm sorry. I went over the top. But I'm all right to go now. Are you ready?"

"Another twenty minutes. But are you sure? Do you need something?"

"No, don't worry, Pete. It was just a bad moment, that's all," I said, getting up and going to the bathroom.

I closed the door behind me, and looked at the reflection of the man in front of me. The image seemed to laugh back at me, and I heard myself say, "Can't go much lower than that, can you Carmichael?"

I turned the tap on, now with water running at last, and threw some water on my face, trying to wash any trace of weakness away. But for a few minutes, I continued to go over my past, in moments of fear and sadness, when I'd go up to my father only to receive a punch on the arm and hear him tell me, *'men shouldn't admit their fears and never show their weaknesses.'*

When I went downstairs to meet the others a little while later, I felt better, because I knew now that what my father had told me then was wrong.

"Sorry, friends," I said to Mike and Bantu. "It's been such a long day."

They both nodded. "Don't worry," Mike said. "I lose it myself, often enough."

"Everyone's ready?" Mbongo asked, looking at Thabo and Bantu loading their pistols before they put them in their shiny belts.

"I'm not real keen on all of this," I said to Mike. It was obvious that we weren't just going to have a cup of coffee with Galijha. And to be honest, I didn't have the faintest idea of what was ahead of us.

No one said anything during the trip, each of us keeping our thoughts to ourselves, and by the time we got to the swamps, night had fallen.

Through the foliage we could make out the almost imperceptible lights of a car. Bantu drove up slowly, but by the time we'd pulled up beside the mysterious vehicle, we found it empty.

There wasn't any obvious explanation, so we stayed where we were in the van, until a short while later, a man appeared from behind some bushes with a jacket hood pulled over his head.

He was carrying a rifle in his right hand but as he approached the vehicle, Thabo got out with his pistol drawn and ordered the hooded figure to stay where he was.

The two men spoke to each other for a while and when the man pulled the hood back, we could see it was Galijha.

"Sorry," he apologized. "But one can't be too careful. If anyone finds out about this meeting, I don't know what will happen."

Peter asked him straight off why he had given us the information at the mine, and what was the actual situation there at the moment.

"A group of investigators came to the mine about a year ago, to do tests on the water there and in the surrounding area. The results never became public, because they didn't live to publish them. The report said they were involved in an accident, not far from here. But that wasn't the case."

I looked into the impenetrable darkness around us and shivered, even though it was warm. There was a big country out there to get conveniently lost in, if you took the wrong turn.

"I guess you thought this was a trap," Galijha said. "And I can't blame you for that, but you can trust me. I've risked my own hide coming here." He paused in the darkness. "I can take you all the way with this, but I need your absolute discretion. Understood?"

There seemed no good reason why he would be lying, so we told him we would keep our part of the deal.

He seemed satisfied. "Follow me."

We got back in the van and followed him for a few minutes through dense scrub until a few miles further ahead where we saw an island of white light in the middle of nowhere. And a second later realized it was Gajha.

He turned his lights off and we followed suit, driving very slowly around the eastern edge of the mine until we came to a halt behind gigantic mounds of rock and gravel, directly behind a sector that was protected by a high, steel fence.

We got out, and caught up to Galijha, who gave us hand torches and precise instructions on how to get to a secret tunnel that would take us, without being seen, right into the heart of the mine.

We followed him silently, like true criminals, using the scrub for cover, conscious of the fact that in the longest stretch we would have to crawl across almost sixty yards without cover, risking being seen by the guards who no doubt would start shooting at shapes that for them were intruders.

We finally hid behind some sand dunes, around five yards from the fence that separated us from our objective. We'd, in effect, reached Sector 38, where we'd seen the men in the cemetery of animals earlier in the day.

Then, to our amazement, Galijha kicked a few rocks out of the way, to reveal a wooden board that was hidden underneath and a hatchway, through which we entered a hole about two feet wide. Galijha told us to turn the torches off and he entered first, followed by Thabo, the three of us, with Bantu at the rear.

Mike who was ahead of me, started to cough, and Pete kicked him and told him to keep quiet, and we continued to follow Galijha in the dark, until we saw a light at the end of the tunnel.

When we got there Galijha slowly pushed a grate open, and stuck his head out to check that no one was around, and as we all came out on the surface, he told us to wait where we were for a while until he gave us the Ok to come out.

He came back a few minutes later and said the area was unpatrolled and Pete and I led the rest of us out.

The grate that covered the tunnel was behind a waste container that kept it well hidden, and leaving the tunnel behind, we followed Galijha in Indian file until we reached the entrance to Sector 38.

The enormous metal lock gates were half open, which surprised Galijha. He said that normally we would have had to enter through the opening of a window that we had to climb up to. But with the lock gates open as they were, he felt somebody could come back at any moment to close them.

We entered, leaving Bantu behind as guard, telling him to knock three times if he saw anyone coming.

After a few yards inside, Thabo separated from the group, exploring another wing of the nave. A fetid stench wrapped itself around us, becoming stronger the further we went. We were all in the grip of a sudden nausea that had us on the point of vomiting. And to complicate matters, we couldn't see anything other than the silhouettes of the metal crates, giant stone drills, a crushing machine and old tractors that seemed to block our way, as if they were threatening giants.

After prowling through the nauseating labyrinth, Galijha ordered us to return the way we'd come and edge our way around the massive things that had stopped us from crossing to the other side.

Suddenly, we heard a scream in the distance that left us petrified. A chill ran right through my body. It had to be Bantu, and we didn't have the faintest idea where he was right then.

Galijha called his name out a few times, but only managed to hear our heavy breathing as we fought to keep calm.

We continued on, rounding the fence of machinery, until we stumbled on a wooden box that was open with two rifles sticking out. Peter bent down and studied the box's contents, peeling back a straw covering and a couple of grey blankets on top of several high caliber weapons.

We looked at each other as Galijha took one of the guns out, checking that it wasn't loaded, and looking at the silencers in the box, told us that what we were looking at wasn't simply a box of security guns.

"It seems like these cretins are covering their backs well," Galijha said. "Now I know why Kassim comes down here several times a week. He's got everything here to carry out his dirty work. I could never have imagined this."

"No? Isn't it obvious that he's in charge of all of this?" I asked.

"I don't know what to think. I've worked for years

with him and thought he was an honourable man. But now, I know that I was wrong. I could never have imagined that he was involved in arms trafficking. I only know that McMahon and Dormonth are his puppets and they do all sorts of dirty work for him. Normally Kassim's never at the plant. He's got other things to do outside Gajha, and when he does show up, he comes straight down here. Now I know why!"

I took my camera out and took some photos of the opened box of rifles. But Galijha suggested we keep going and a few steps farther on, we could see through the darkness, a great pit, around six yards in diameter, and from out of which we heard what seemed like someone in agony, groaning.

We ran to the edge and flashed our torches into the blackness, but could see nothing. It was too deep. We called Thabo again and a few seconds later heard his agonizing voice from the dim hollow.

"I can't move. Can't move," he repeated. "My legs are broken. And the stench here is unbearable. I'm going to die here."

"No, you're not going to die here," Galijha called out. "Just hang on. We'll go and get something to get you out of there."

"Don't let me die here alone…" the forlorn voice from below begged us. "There's something terrible down here. I can't see what, I lost my torch. It's sticky, and it's like everything's full of hairs and wooden sticks. And all this glue has covered my legs. I don't know what it is, but it's awful," he started coughing compulsively.

We all directed our lights inside the pit, until a funereal silence reigned again. Seconds later, Thabo screamed out in horror. "My God, it's hell down here.

I can't believe it. Don't leave me here. Don't leave me here. It's a swamp..., a swamp of blood."

I looked at the others and said: "Shit, that's just all we needed."

"It's full of dead animals," he called out, "and a human foot! How did that get here?"

"Calm down, Thabo. We'll get you out soon, man," Mike reassured him.

Peter took out his camera and started filming, the tele-lens getting a close up of what was happening down below. "Christ..." Peter grunted, looking through the lens. "I can't believe this..., poor bastard. It's the worst thing I've ever seen. Let's get him out of there fast."

"We'll get a rope. Just hang on. We'll be back soon," Galijha called out, but lowering his voice he said to us, "If they surprise us here they'll kill us all."

Thabo went silent while Galijha told us to find Bantu and tell him what happened while he'd stay behind to guard Thabo. He took a gun out and started looking for a hiding place.

"Let's go," Pete said, as we turned and ran towards the entrance.

As we saw Bantu standing by the gate with a grin of relief, this soon erased from his face when he heard the bad news. We ran towards the tunnel, and as we were about to get inside, we heard the roar of an engine coming our way.

We got out of there as quickly as we could, scrambling through the tunnel to the other side of the fence and looking back from the other side, we could see a huge tractor heading for where Galijha and Thabo were.

Bantu was repeating some sort of mantra in Swahili

as we ran back to the van, and kept repeating it all the way back to the ranch.

Mbongo was standing in front of the house when we arrived. It seemed he'd guessed that something was wrong.

"By the look of you, things didn't work out too well, didn't they?" he said.

"Thabo fell in a hole and is badly injured, Captain," Bantu informed him. "We need a rope to get him out. The man who took us there stayed behind to guard him. I… I don't know what's going to happen."

"Don't waste time," Mbongo ordered in a grave voice, walking inside. He handed us a powerful steel lamp, a length of rope and hastened us sullenly. "Get moving. But no more mistakes."

"But Thabo's legs are broken," Peter said. "How are we going to get him out of there, if he can't walk?"

"Follow me," Mbongo replied, walking to the rear garden. "Here are some wooden planks. Take what you need and make a splint. You should be able to carry or drag him on those."

We took two of the planks and without further delay returned to Gajha.

As we drove there, I went over everything that had happened. I couldn't believe it and couldn't get the sound of Thabo's groaning out of my head. Besides, we had no real idea of how we were going to get him out of that hole and back through the tunnel to the van.

We scrambled through the long tunnel and came out the other side of the fence, where, to our surprise, we found the warehouse open and the light on inside. We gave each other a shared look of doubt and walked nervously up to one of the small windows, from where we could see more lights on inside and hear the loud roar of engines, coming and going.

Things had turned for the worse, if that was possible.

We tiptoed in and followed the deafening noise along the long corridor that led to where Thabo had fallen.

Two tractors were pouring gigantic shovels full of stone, metal and limestone into the hole. Peter took his camera out and started to take a series of quick photos that would no doubt comprise the crucial part of the report.

Unexpectedly and leaving us all stunned, we saw Mike running out without warning and tried to get the tractor drivers to stop pouring their loads into the abyss, where sometime before, Thabo had been lying in agony.

We just watched stupefied as the drivers paid no attention to Mike's desperate calls to desist what they were doing, and then watched in horror as one of them pulled a rifle out, pointed it, and fired. Mike reeled back with the impact, and collapsed in a heap on the ground.

CHAPTER
NINE

In the middle of the confusion, I charged out in Mike's direction, grabbed him by the jacket and started dragging him away, in the middle of a gunfight that was underway now between the mine worker and Bantu. I managed to get Mike under a water pump, and seconds later, dragged him farther away from the bullets with Pete's help.

"Get out of here!" Bantu yelled. "I'll take care of this. Just run as fast as you can."

Pete, regardless of the danger and the possible tragedy built into the scene, continued to film, getting as much action as he could into the camera.

"This is just what we needed," Pete alleged, as I looked around for some sign of Galijha, and to my horror, I saw a lifeless body in the arm of a tractor waiting to be thrown into the crater of the sacrificed.

Still crouching and firing, Bantu tried to distract the shooters away from us, as somehow, I carried Mike on my back towards the tunnel that would take us out of the mine.

Mike had been shot in the shoulder, and I couldn't make too much sense out of what he was saying; at one moment he wanted to die, and the next, he'd never give up.

I don't know how I found the strength to carry him. It had to be a burst of adrenaline rushing through my veins.

I put him down when we got to the tunnel, because there wasn't enough room for the two of us moving the way we were. I went in first and Pete eased Mike in after me and I pulled him the whole length of a tunnel that this time seemed to be a mile long. I collapsed in a heap at the other end, my lungs at the point of bursting.

With Pete's help I got Mike back to the van and put him in the back seat. He'd lost a lot of blood and Pete did the best he could to stop the hemorrhaging, plugging the wound with a bandage and gauzes that he took from the first-aid box. We had no way of knowing if he was going to live or die. Pete just drove as fast as he could towards the ranch, both of us speechless and in shock.

Pete broke the silence halfway there. "How could we have been so stupid to fall into the middle of all of this?"

I said nothing, because I was too exhausted to speak and because I knew he was right. I watched him punch the dashboard with his fist. "How could we have been so naive to think that we could just take as many photos as we wanted to, and then simply walk out again? I can only hope that the photos we did take will sink those bastards, and put them where they belong."

The lights were on at the front door of the house when we finally made it back with Mbongo standing there, with a look of disgust on his face as he watched

Pete and I carry Mike in. "That's all I needed. What happened? Where are Thabo and Bantu?"

When we didn't answer him, he turned his attention to his wife and daughter who he ordered to come immediately with water and towels, a bottle of brandy, forceps and needle and thread. And turning back to Peter, he told him to get a flask of amber liquid that was on the kitchen shelf.

Christ, I thought. Mbongo's the surgeon!

I tried to convince myself that he knew what he was doing, and got my mind off what was going on by telling him what had happened. "Everything went bad, Captain, much worse than we could've imagined. When we got there they'd already buried Thabo and Galijha under a ton of rocks and limestone."

I collapsed onto the rocking chair in the corner and went over the scene again. "There was a gunfight. That's how Mike was wounded. And Thabo told us to get out of there. I don't know what's happened to him."

Mbongo glared in complete silence; he had his hands full, pouring the bottle of brandy into Mike's mouth. I thought he was going to choke on the brandy. He could barely swallow.

I wanted to stop Mbongo but he turned his cold, black eyes on me and said, "I know what I'm doing, John. I need your friend to lose consciousness or that close to it that he doesn't know what's going on. Taking a bullet out of a man's not that easy, you know."

Pete walked up to the captain, uncorked the amber bottle and placed it on the table. He stayed where he was, watching how Mbongo finished getting Mike drunk.

Mike had drunk the best part of half a bottle of brandy and ingested a couple of pain killers that the captain had put in his mouth to lessen the pain. His head was drooping like a rag doll. "Steady him!" Mbongo told us. "I need to clean the wound first."

We held Mike as tight as we could and when everything was as ready as it could be, Mbongo poured the rest of the brandy over the wound, and inserted the point of a pair of forceps into the breach in Mike's shoulder, extracting the bullet at the very moment that Mike gave out a scream that made my hair stand on end. The tension left Mike's body almost immediately, as he lost consciousness.

"That's better," Mbongo said, nodding his approval.

He wet a towel with the amber liquid from the bottle, and then stitched the wound with needle and thread. He looked more like a man sewing a turkey up after stuffing it, than he did a doctor going about his work. And with each stitch, Mike's skin was stretched right out, like a piece of elastic to the point of ripping, before being returned to his shoulder. I felt like vomiting, so I closed my eyes to calm down only to open them again, with Mike's next scream.

The Captain finished up and Pete brought a blanket and pillow down from the bedroom and we laid Mike down in the sofa, where he'd spend the rest of the night.

Mbongo slumped into the rocking chair, Mike on another chair, and I stretched out on the armchair, without being able to take my eyes off Mike. We stayed like that until the next morning, when the dawn light filtered through the old, wooden Persian blinds.

During most of the night I couldn't stop thinking about Bantu's fate and everything else that had happened. And when I did get chances to nod off, I'd be woken again by Mike, who seemed to alternate between dreams and hallucinations, his body and the blanket covered in sweat. The three of us taking turns at wiping him down with cold towels to alleviate the nightmare he was going through.

And he didn't seem to wake up any better either, almost without strength, opening and closing his eyes with a lost look on his face.

The captain checked the wound to make sure it wasn't infected, and although it was inflamed, he said that it seemed to be all right. So, we carried Mike up to the bedroom where he could rest without being bothered for the rest of the day.

To add to our bad luck, there was no village or town nearby where we could get antibiotics, so the captain suggested that we go the next day to Gambala, where Mike could be checked by the doctor or the Reserve veterinarian.

I liked the idea, the thought of seeing Marie again, putting a smile on my face.

"But today we'll stay here," Mbongo said. "We need to find out what happened to Bantu. And it's more than likely that if he did get away, they'll be out looking for him everywhere."

"We should call the police," I suggested. "People can't just go around killing people whenever they want. We owe it to both Galijha and Thabo to not let this go uninvestigated. Besides we don't know where Bantu is."

"And we won't until he appears," Pete said. "John's right, Captain, we should report this to the authorities."

Mbongo shook his head. "I'm afraid that's impossible, boys. It's very likely the mine has got the police and the Government and God knows who else in their pocket. We're surrounded by unscrupulous people."

It was clear that Mbongo knew more than we did about how things worked in Tanzania. And I suspected that he'd had firsthand experience with corrupt police. He asked his wife to bring three cups of tea and went over to a cupboard whose doors appeared to be coming off their hinges, opened a drawer and pulled out an envelope that had turned yellow with time. Then walked back and sat down again.

The expression on his face had changed, no doubt brought on by the handful of photos that he took out of the envelope. His eyes clouded over, and he entered a deep and what appeared to be melancholic silence, as he stared at one photo in particular. "See this young man," he said, turning the photo to us. "This was my boy. He was a decent man, a good father, a good son and excellent worker. A true gentleman, who gave his life for those he loved. Both his mother and I were proud to be his parents."

I didn't want to ask what had happened to his son and just hoped that he would tell us when he was ready. Mbongo's chin was trembling, but the words came out. "It was only eight months ago that he was killed. Just after one of his many trips to a town near Lake Victoria. He'd just come back from the shore of the lake. He was bringing some fertilizer back to the ranch for the fertilizing season and the fumigation of the tea plantation." Mbongo sighed, put the photo down on the table. His chest was heaving, but the chin was firm now. "Along the way he'd seen dozens of dead animals and birds. They'd just ceased to exist as if some massive explosion had happened or some freak event of nature had occurred. But my son knew there was another reason"

"He'd found out a lot about the mine's activities and informed the authorities. They appeared to be interested and asked him to take them to where he'd found all the dead animals. Naively, he thought he was doing good, but he could never have imagined that he was talking his way into his own murder. But that's what happened. And those bastards, posing as health inspectors killed him in the very spot where all the other animals and birds lay dead. And they just left my son there, floating in the water, until his almost unrecognizable body was found two weeks later. That's what happens from trying to do things right around here. The law just washed its hands of the affair, claimed he was killed by his best friend in a drunken argument."

He stopped for a while, sipped some tea, and then went on. "That young man, who I've known since he first began to walk, is paying for a crime he didn't commit. They made him the scapegoat for one of their most hideous crimes. They made up a story about him threatening my son years ago, about getting married to his sister. That girl's my daughter-in-law today and the mother of my three grandchildren." He paused. "Around here the good ones die and evil triumphs." He took the envelope back to the cupboard, put it back in the drawer and walked away, but half-turned near the door, to warn us to be careful in the next few days because the hyenas were loose and looking for prey.

CHAPTER
TEN

I felt like I had an emotional hangover the next morning when I woke up, thoughts of my own past confused with the events of the last few days. I couldn't get Thabo's cruel death out of my mind, saw him under an avalanche of rocks, screaming, and Galijha shoveled in to join him in that gruesome, deathly pit. Were their deaths in vain? The cause was noble, but would any action change a land where corruption and evil was endemic? And what had happened to Bantu? Had he met the same grisly fate, too? I tried to let my thoughts settle on the possibility of him escaping, saw him walking back to the ranch, across the savanna, wounded maybe, but still with his life intact, a future ahead of him. It was better to think of Bantu, and not that dark abyss where so many animals and at least two humans had died.

I went up with Pete to Mike's room, hoping that he'd slept well, and was about to make a remarkable recovery that would see us go on with the trip as we'd planned. I was sure that was what we all wanted, and hoped that he would not only be able to do that, but that he'd return to his wife in England without any further problems. I knew Sarah wouldn't be able to take any more bad news.

"Rest, Mike," Pete said, placing his hand on Mike's shoulder. "Tomorrow we're going to Gambala where you'll have your wound looked at properly."

"That's right, Mike. Don't make me get angry again like you did yesterday," I said, grinning.

"No, no, Carmichael," Pete joked, putting both hands up and grimacing. "We don't want that again, old boy, do we?"

I laughed. "Why did I bring it up? You'll never let me forget it."

Mike and Pete started laughing, and after a few more jokes, most of them centred on me, Pete and I packed the bags.

Lunch was nothing like the other days. Pete, the captain and I, looked glum, sitting at a table full of food that would have been tempting under any other circumstances. The excitement of our arrival had been forgotten and none of us wanted to talk about the day before. So we ate in silence.

After lunch, I told the others I was going for a walk around the property. I felt like taking some photos of something eye-catching, perhaps a baobab tree, a Mpingo, the African Blackwood, or anything to get my mind off what had happened. The captain took a pistol out of his jacket and gave it to me. "Be careful, John," he warned. "We don't know what's coming our way today!"

"But Captain?" I looked at the gun in my hands

without knowing what to say. But after what seemed like a minute's silence, I stuck it in the back of my pants and walked down the wooden staircase, out into the plantation.

I just walked and walked, without any idea where I was going, trying to get a grip on my feelings, to turn myself back from the dark visions that pervaded my mind.

I thought about the fragility of life, and the cruelty of humans. The two seemed incompatible. Surely, life should be revered, not taken in the way it had been the day before. And thinking about what had happened brought back the feeling of impotence that I'd felt then, staring down into that hell, that tangle of blood, animals and my own kind. But as I walked on, my fury was slowly tempered by the warm African breeze and I swung the camera off my shoulder, and began photographing the landscape. I was feeling better, and a little while later, rounding a tree, I came to a clearing where I could see two men in the distance with long ropes taming a horse. The chestnut was bucking wildly, while behind the field, another colt was tied to a tree, waiting its turn. I walked up to the fence attracted by the scene and climbed up and sat there, without the men being aware of my presence, watching the horse jumping and bucking, trying to dislodge the rider from his saddle.

Without realizing it, this African rodeo had put a smile on my face. My mood here on the fence, camera in hand, had lightened even more. I stayed there for a long while watching them taming the spirited animal, and then finally got down and continued on, without having any idea where I was going or what I would see next.

The sky clouded over, turning grey, but no rain fell,

and despite the sun beginning to set, it seemed to be even hotter than before. I felt exhausted, began to walk more slowly, aware of the feeling that I didn't want to go back to the ranch, and go over, once again, what had happened the night before. I realized I wanted the trip to end, to return to my old cat Morris and see my sister again.

I crossed the field, weaving slowly between bushes and trees that seemed to be struggling to stay alive in this infernal drought that had lasted months, when I suddenly sensed that I was being followed.

I stopped and looked behind me, but saw nothing. There were trees and bushes everywhere, and glancing to my left and right, I tried to discern shapes behind branches, but couldn't see anything. I took a deep breath and decided to continue my way back, and around the next tree, I saw the lights of the ranch in the distance. Suddenly, a dry branch snapped behind me in the dark. I froze, took the gun out from under my belt, and turned around slowly. "Come out from where you are, you coward," I yelled.

I had no way of knowing what was stalking me. I was in Africa after all. But I could feel the adrenalin surging through me again, like it had the night before.

Everything was quiet again, which only intensified the feeling that I was being watched. I was the prey and my heart was pounding in my chest, my breathing heavy, I could hear myself panting, and a burst of fury broke me out of the sensation of being corralled, as I'd had the night before. I fired a shot in the air, ready for whatever was out there and seconds later, I felt my legs give way beneath me, and my head crash into the ground, with two men on my back like two hyenas, one with his elbow on my neck, while the other put the boot in, before one heavy blow to the head knocked me out.

CHAPTER
ELEVEN

A painful drumming in my head brought me back to a cloudy consciousness. It was dark and everything seemed to be thumping inside me. I discovered that I was gagged with my hands tied, flat on the floor of an open top utility van, rattling along a road.

I dragged myself up and saw Gajha in the distance. With a great effort, I edged my way to the cabin window. Two Africans were inside, arguing in an incomprehensible dialect, referring to me constantly as *the Englishman*. It didn't sound or look good, and the thought of visiting Gajha a second time, was something I needed to avoid at all costs.

The vehicle was traveling at speed, the road still clear enough to allow the driver to put his foot down. The mine was the devil, and throwing myself over the side of the van was the deep blue sea, but what other choice did I have? I had to do something quick, or it would be too late. So I gulped some air in, made my way to the edge, and thinking about that horrible pit full of dead animals and human bodies in the mine ahead, I hurled myself over the side, hitting the road like a block of cement, pain surging through my ankle.

I couldn't stand up, but managed, with my hands still tied, to get myself into the cover of the bushes. A low branch above me helped me lift myself up and I put weight on my foot, testing it. It was better than I'd first thought, good enough to run, which is what I did without a seconds delay.

I wanted to get as far away from Gajha as I could, but fell over several times, dragging myself up like a man in a straight-jacket, cursing. My worst fears were confirmed a few minutes later, when I saw the lights of a vehicle coming back down the road from the mine. I dashed into some scrub, and a while later a van sped past my hiding place. There was little doubt that it was the two men, and I supposed they were heading back to the ranch. But that was where I had to go to and I figured I'd worry about them when the time came.

I don't know how long I ran for, because I was lost in the effort of running, and the blind determination to get back. But after what must have been an hour or more, I saw the entrance to the ranch and the van with the two Africans inside, parked in front.

I stopped, and exhausted from the effort, hid again in some bushes, more conscious now of the pain in my ankle. I lay down, cursing ever having come to Tanzania in the first place, and wondering whether I'd ever get out of the country in one piece.

I spent the next hour grumbling to myself, until the sun began to rise on the horizon. My foot seemed suddenly worse, as the boot had tightened around the ankle. I wanted to scream from the pain, but bit on a branch instead, and a short time later, and no doubt prompted by daylight, the van drove off.

"Bloody bastards!" I cursed them under my breath, as I dragged myself up and limped back along the track to the ranch.

I don't know how I managed to get there, but when I did, I found Mbongo and Pete armed, with their guns sticking through the windows. They charged out of the house to help me, firing a fusillade of questions that I didn't have the strength to answer.

On seeing me in the state I was in, Mbongo stopped talking, and ordered a man standing at the front door to bring a knife. And when the stranger came back, I realized it was Bantu. "Bantu!" I gasped. "You're alive, man!"

"And you barely," he said, kneeling down at my side.

"I felt so bad about leaving you back there the other night."

"Don't give it another thought. What's important is that we're both here now," he said. "But I don't want to talk about that now. Thabo was like a brother to me," he bent down as far as the boot, slipped the knife inside and eased it open. I stifled a scream, as the blood flowed freely again, and the pain stormed back.

"I'm sorry, Mister John," he apologized. "But there's no other way to get the boot off. Your foot's very swollen."

"Don't worry, Bantu," I told him, as I leaned forward, head down, my teeth clenched, as the others looked grimly on, and after the boot was off, I limped with Pete and Bantu's help towards the house.

Mike leaned out of a window above. "Boy, I am glad you made it back."

I nodded, and before entering the house lifted my head up and asked him. "And you? How are you faring?"

"I'm still here," he called back, shrugging his shoulders as I went in.

The Captain's wife was in the living room with a towel under her arm and a bucket of hot water doused with salt. I sat down in an armchair and with her help, slowly put my foot into the bucket. It took a while to get accustomed to the boiling water, but soon after the pain began to go down.

But now, with one pain under control, I discovered that the blow to my head had produced a lump the size of a camel's hump, just above my forehead, and while my foot soaked in the water, I rubbed my head softly for almost an hour, while I told the others what had happened. They just sat there amazed.

"You're lucky to be alive, Carmichael," Pete said. "We had no idea what happened to you last night. We were out there for hours looking for you."

I just nodded and could see clearly from the expression on Peter's face that he felt we still weren't out of danger. "These bastards are hunting us down, mate. It's not over yet."

I changed the subject. "And how's Mike? He didn't look that good."

"Up and down," Mbongo said. "Fortunately, the wound seems to be healing quite well. He slept better and the fever broke... but..."

"But what?" I asked.

"The bullet was heading towards the collar bone and it seems to have affected a nerve. The arm's weak and he doesn't have much feeling in his left hand. I hope it's just swollen but he needs to rest. So he's still in the room. The sooner you get to Gambala the better. Bantu will take you there along a back road. You shouldn't have any problems along the way."

I thought about Gambala and the condition I was in.

"The doctor in the Reserve will have a look at you both," Mbongo said. "Besides, you'll need time to build your strength back up before you return to London."

Mbongo's words made sense, and the thought of getting out of the hell that we were now in, and back to London, put a smile on my face. But it wasn't as simple as that. I knew and I was sure that Pete and Mike did, too, but at the same time, many people were depending on us. A lot of money had been spent getting us and our equipment to Tanzania, so we had no other choice than to finish our report, one way or the other.

After sleeping most of the morning and well into the afternoon, I was suddenly woken by a wild storm. I was still lying on the living room couch. Struggling to stand up, I walked to the window, where I saw a wall of water, pushed by a strong wind, slicing diagonally across the dark sky. Moments later, Mbongo appeared with a worried look on his face. "This is all I need," he said. "If this keeps up, it's the end of the tea crop!"

His wife came up to him and said nervously, as she was trying to tie her apron up. "I haven't seen rain like this for a long time. Remember, eight years ago?"

Mbongo nodded. "Yes, and the wet season hasn't even started yet!"

The storm continued for many hours. The entire house seemed to be leaking, as everyone worked overtime, carrying buckets and plastic containers to be filled by rainwater that seeped through the moth-eaten ceilings. And then, as if a magician had waved his wand, it suddenly stopped, and everyone returned to their rooms, exhausted.

I decided to spend the rest of the night downstairs, as I didn't want to bother Mike who was still recovering very slowly. I sighed and looked out on the clearest night sky I could ever remember seeing. It seemed like the whole universe was out there, lined up for me to see.

I staggered back to the sofa, my whole body aching, but touched by the infinity of stars above me, I fell asleep until dawn, when I was woken by a loud commotion at the back of the house.

CHAPTER
TWELVE

I looked at a pair of brown leather sandals under the table, while listening to the ruckus outside. Pain and exhaustion begged me to stay in bed, but curiosity's a powerful thing. I looked at my ankle before I put any weight on it, and deciding it had improved, I stood up tentatively, slipped the sandals on, and limping, made my way to the back yard. A large group of people were looking out on what appeared to be the almost total destruction of the plantation.

Visibly moved, Mbongo was standing next to his wife and daughter, his eyes closed, praying in silence, before he looked at the shaken faces of the workers around him. "The earth is noble," he said, opening his eyes. "It will recover soon and in spite of everything, there will be a new beginning. We'll start over again. Don't give up hope. Remember that this is the way life is. There are good years and bad years. The sooner we get back to work and clean everything up, the closer we'll be to that new beginning."

Leaving Mbongo below with the workers, Pete and I went upstairs to Mike's room. He was still in bed, staring through the window, deep in thought. He looked tired and there was a flicker of pain in his expression, even though he seemed to have recovered well enough.

"What's happening downstairs?" he asked.

"Yesterday's storm destroyed most of the plantation," I told him. "You can imagine the impact that's had on Mbongo and the workers."

Mike didn't answer, just looked at my foot, closed his eyes for a few seconds then said. "The sooner we leave this place, the better. It's been one disaster after another round here."

He got out of bed and started getting dressed, struggling to pull his trousers on with his right hand. Obviously frustrated, he threw them on the floor and kicked the table; his eyes were glassy and his chin trembling. "You know what I think," he said in a dark voice that didn't seem to be his. "When we signed the contract to come here, we signed our own death warrant. Those bastards out there won't let up until they've killed us all."

"Take it easy, Mike," Pete said, standing in front of him and helping him to get dressed. "We'll be on our way to Gambala soon. Everything will be different there."

At half-past twelve we were downstairs on the porch, sitting on the steps, in silence, surrounded by our bags and the equipment, waiting for the van.

"Look!" Pete said, pointing at a cloud of dust in the distance, as a vehicle sped through the entrance to the ranch, and a minute later, Bantu jumped out. "Put everything in quick! We've got to go now!"

CHAPTER
THIRTEEN

Bantu waved his hands wildly in the air and screamed. "Get in now! Let's go! A convoy of vehicles from the mine is heading this way. It looks like they're going to blame us for what happened last night. They're armed and I don't think they're going to listen to explanations."

"Blame us?" Pete said in disgust. "You must be joking. They killed Thabo and Galijha, and were on the point of killing you and Mike and John. You can't be serious."

"There's no time to talk it through. Just get in! And hurry!" Mbongo said, helping us load everything on. "Don't waste any more time. If they come here, I'll tell them you left last night. Now get out of here!"

"Thanks for everything, Captain. I hope someday we can pay you back for everything you've done for us. Say goodbye to your wife and daughter," I said, slamming the van door behind me, as we took off along a track behind the ranch that led to a deserted road that would take us across country without being seen.

It was a rough ride, veering through fallen trees, broken branches and others on the point of snapping; a veritable path of destruction that had been left by the storm from the night before.

"What a disaster," Bantu said, shaking his head. "I can't believe it. With everything that's happened here, you must be praying to get back to London. These men don't play games and they won't let up until they make someone pay for their own mistakes."

There was no doubt that Bantu was right, and we sat grimfaced in the car, going over everything that had happened, as the bumpy ride from hell continued. Slowing down, Bantu said, "I don't know if you know what happened in the mine yesterday, after all that rain?" Mike, who had been sitting there with his eyes closed for the last few miles, no doubt trying to forget everything, suddenly opened them. "What happened, Bantu?"

"It was on the radio. The mine walls collapsed, burying dozens of miners underneath."

"I can't believe it," I said, shocked, before asking sarcastically. "Anything else to report, friend? Maybe Kiliminjaro's collapsed?"

"No, Mister John, the mountain's still there."

"Well, you know what I mean, Bantu. Is it always like this around here?"

"Well, not always," he answered. "But to tell you the truth, there hasn't been much peace around here for years."

"And what happened in the mines?" Pete asked.

"They say there's little chance of finding them alive."

"Poor bastards," Mike said, closing his eyes again. "That's awful..., poor families."

"I'm with you," Pete agreed. "They're victims of negligence. The management doesn't implement the right controls. They don't calculate the risks and when something like this happens, they just wash their hands of the whole thing. Blame it on a storm. Why didn't they get the miners out of there when it started pelting down? Or even an hour after that?"

No one said anything else for a few minutes until Bantu brought the van to a halt when we came to a crossing. "Before we continue to Gambala, I'll take you to the shore at Lake Victoria. I think you'll find it very interesting."

"And if we're seen?" I asked.

"I don't think there'll be anyone there at this time of day," he said, leaning on the steering wheel. "But it's something you've got to see before you go."

His words were convincing, so we turned towards Urekewe, and a half an hour later parked the van thirty yards from the shore. "Keep close behind," Bantu said, leading off with Pete and I following, carrying the cameras. Mike stayed behind where he was.

The track was full of flies and insects that buzzed around the sweat on our faces, as we walked, blinding us. I started flailing my shoulders and head like a religious zealot, as I felt them biting into me. And when I wasn't battling them, or cursing, I was thinking malaria. A few minutes later, and a foul stench hit us hard. I felt like vomiting, but forced myself to keep up, as Bantu led us along a track that wound its way through spiny brush, the stench getting stronger the further we went.

We finally came out on a Dantesque scene that made us gasp. A dead crocodile was floating in the shallows, a pack of scavenger birds on its stomach, picking its entrails, and on the shore itself, a large horned, black-faced wildebeest and a swollen zebra that looked on the point of bursting, lay among other animals that had been ravaged by predators.

We walked in circles through the horrific scene, until the almost inaudible groans of a small black shape in the distance made us stop. I couldn't make it out at first, but as I moved closer, I spotted a small baboon in its death throes. It wasn't any more than a few weeks old, and its mother lay a few yards away in a total state of decomposition. I walked up slowly to the tiny monkey with the black head and pink mask, which appeared to be unaware of my presence. Its black eyes were veiled and it looked at me with a sadness that was heart wrenching. It looked as if tears were running down its cheeks, and it moved its hands as if imploring me to help.

I quickly bent down, took my safari jacket off and wrapped it inside. It whimpered painfully, I held it in my arms, a thread of blood dripping from its mouth onto its chest. It was so moving. The animal, only a baby, now an orphan, innocently was facing its own death. I felt a cold fury against those responsible for such an atrocious crime, and the irresponsibility of man in causing such suffering.

With the baby baboon in my arms, I dragged my leg painfully back to where Peter was looking at me curiously, slowly lowering his camera. "I'm going back to the van. I've seen enough here."

He nodded, and finished filming the apocalypse on the lakeshore. Ten minutes later we resumed our trip to Gambala.

We were all shaken, and remained silent during the

rest of the trip, while the baby baboon rested its head weakly on my chest.

It seemed to me that we'd never get to the Reserve on time, and I had the feeling that the tiny animal would die in my arms. I took the canteen out of the backpack and tried to give it some water, but there seemed to be an obstruction in its throat that didn't let it swallow a drop. Helplessly, I heard it let out almost inaudible whimpers, shaking its tiny hands.

About an hour later we arrived at the arid entrance to the Reserve. But as we drove on, the landscape gradually changed; a stream, watering dense jungle, lined the way. It was a true oasis, in the middle of a parched savanna, where animals roamed peacefully on both sides of the track.

When we got to the camp, I asked the first person I saw, where I could find Marie. Her clinic was in a pavilion at the end of a long corridor, where dozens of animals were kept in cages. I put the baby baboon on the stainless steel bench in the centre of the room and a while later Marie appeared at the door, staring at the tiny animal, lying there quivering, almost unable to breathe.

She ran to a shelf laden with bottles of saline solution, cotton balls and alcohol, and came back to the table with a catheter that she fitted on one of its little arms. She took a pocket lamp out and looked into its eyes, in its mouth and enormous pink ears. Then from a cabinet with glass doors, she selected a blister from the dozens that were lined in rows inside.

She came back to the table and extracted the contents of the blister with an insulin syringe, took the baboon's leg, rubbed it with cotton, and injected it in the thigh. The poor creature was too weak to even react to the prick of the needle.

Marie looked at me in silence for a few seconds, immersed in her own thoughts, when I saw her click her fingers and go to a table where there were more bottles. She grabbed one that held a pinkish liquid and, extracting a little with a syringe without a needle, she introduced it slowly into the little baboon's mouth, until after a few attempts, it managed to swallow it all.

With a sigh of relief, a vague expression of satisfaction covered Marie's face. She lifted the animal up in her hands, opened one of the cages with a sheepskin base and laid it down carefully inside, adjusted the drip of the solution and patting its cheek, she whispered to it in a maternal voice. "You'll get well soon, little girl."

"Little girl?" I said, raising my eyebrow.

"Yes, it's a girl," she said, drawing a sparkling smile.

"And do you think she'll recover?"

"I hope so, John."

I felt a sudden burst of pleasure on hearing my name coming out of those lips. It was more than nice to be remembered.

"What happened to your foot?" she asked, her attention attracted by the bandage. "You've had a hard time by the look of it."

I grimaced. "I'll tell you later. At dinner?"

"Sure, see you then, John," she said, as she walked off, leaving me in the room alone, surrounded by cages.

I looked at the animals inside more closely. Almost all of them were babies: a pair of small baboons was sleeping on top of each other; three black-faced vervet monkeys were playing, biting each other's tails; a young chimpanzee was banging his plastic plate against the bars of a cage. I felt sorry for them all, locked up here, away from their natural habitat where now their lives were in danger.

I heard someone walking quickly along the corridor and turned to see Phillipe come into the room with a radio in his hand. He was as surprised to see me standing there by the cages, as I was to see him. It was more than obvious that he wasn't pleased with my presence there. He didn't say a word, just went to his desk, took some folders out and left through the same door he'd entered from.

It wasn't going to be easy to work my way around Phillipe's apparent jealousy, but there was plenty of incentive to bide my time. I knew well enough that overreacting wasn't the answer, and wouldn't go down well with Marie, either. I walked out a few minutes later to look for the others who were settling into one of the pavilions. The pathway to our new quarters was lined on both sides by cages that housed hundreds of primates of all ages, jumping from one branch to the next inside, grunting and chasing even younger terrified monkeys, with chunks of fruit in their mouths.

The sun was setting, painting the afternoon sky orange and violet, until it disappeared over the horizon.

So much had happened in such a short time that I still hadn't had time to digest it all. I observed my surroundings more carefully, the colours sharper and more intense. I listened to the crickets, and while standing there, strangely open to everything, I became conscious that I'd been close to dying, and here now, everything that lived and breathed, was brushed anew by the colours of dusk. The fulcrum of my life had shifted.

I suddenly understood Pete and Mike's innate sensitivity and their deep appreciation of a world that I hadn't been able to perceive, or rather, hadn't wanted to perceive.

I saw Mummbar in the distance; he waved and came over with a solemn expression on his face. "I'm sorry John. I could never have imagined that all of this would've happened to you. Peter's told me a little bit about it," he said, turning to look at Pete talking to someone standing outside what would be our dorm quarters. "It was very risky to go back to the mine at night. It's a miracle that you're still alive to talk about it."

I didn't feel like talking anymore about the subject, so kept silent. He seemed to understand. "Come with me," he said. "I want to introduce you to Bill Turner. He's the founder and head of Gambala. He's English, too, but was brought up in Germany. He's a renowned conservationist, who together with the organization that he himself founded, and which bears the same name as the Reserve, has devoted himself to raising funds to carry out this project. He's also done a great job in the local communities which receive information and environmental education. We promote, on the one hand, social awareness, and on the other, we create job opportunities that generate income without damaging the region's biodiversity."

"Interesting," I said, as we walked up to Turner, a heavily-built balding man with a thick, unruly moustache that completely covered his upper lip.

"Pleased to meet you, I'm John Carmichael," I said, extending my hand.

"The pleasure's mine," he answered in a hoarse voice, shaking my hand firmly and looking me square in the eyes. "Make yourself at home here. Have a rest if you like before afternoon tea."

"Thanks, Sir..."

"Call me Bill," he said, before he walked off.

After he'd gone, Pete and I walked inside the

pavilion, where Mike was sleeping on a clapped-out metal folding bed. After unpacking and making as little noise as we could, we left the room to meet Turner and Mummbar, who we found sitting in a porch room at the entrance to the main building.

They were talking about the damage caused by the storm the night before. On seeing us arrive, they invited us into a large room that looked like a university cafeteria. We sat down at a table of exotic African rosewood called anigre, and Mummbar offered us a glass of a strong liqueur called Konyagi, typical of the region, which he poured from a bottle on the table. As we sipped the liqueur, we told them in detail about what had happened in the last few days.

While Pete and I were explaining what had happened Phillipe came in, greeted everyone, except me, sat down and served himself a Konyagi, which prompted Mummbar to refill ours. It was a strange mix, telling the dark tale of the last few days, while we drank this powerful gin-like liqueur, which helped us unwind.

"Taking everything into account, I think we've got enough film to make a very good documentary," Pete said. "We've been filming all the way through, even in the thick of the action. And I'm not talking just about film of ecological damage. We've got plenty more as well."

Mummbar raised his glass. "It makes me very happy to have you here. And to hear what you've told us. In the next few days the doctor will treat your injuries and get you back to full health so you can continue your work."

Turner brought us back to the present. "We've got to be very careful with these criminals. And I hope they haven't discovered your tracks. For the moment you're safe here in the Reserve."

That was reassuring to hear, and I imagined an oasis of peace in a violent world.

"We'll try and fix everything so that your work can continue as soon as possible," Turner explained. "Tomorrow you can see the work that Dr. Dubois and her team are doing. Read their reports; check the health of the animals. We'll also give you detailed information about the surrounding areas. We'll take you there sometime tomorrow."

I could see we were going to be busy, and wondered when Marie would have time get round to treating me. Turner turned his attention to Phillipe, telling him to have all the laboratory test results available, as well as the water analysis measurement results from various parts of Lake Victoria, which had shown the presence of toxic substances, like sodium cyanide, lead, mercury, cadmium and arsenic among others.

"It's a pity," he said, looking at all of us, "that we don't have the adequate technology to be able to measure these contaminants precisely."

Mummbar joined in. "We'll also go to neighboring villages where we'll interview the sick and the families who have lost loved ones, and who are of course against the mine's activities."

Turner interrupted him. "I promise you that you won't be placed in any more danger. I think you've been through enough for one trip."

I wanted to shout my agreement, but the cook appeared at the door, and Turner said something to her, before turning back to us. "But we'll leave all the other business for tomorrow. You need to relax now and enjoy traditional Tanzanian cooking. We'll serve Mike in his room."

"Speaking about food," Mummbar said, his black

eyes gleaming, "our cook's the best there is around here. I don't know what we'd do without her."

Both Pete and I smiled, but I really wanted to scream. The heat and the effort of walking and standing up since the morning had cut my blood circulation and the throbbing in my foot had gone from waltz to heavy metal. I had the feeling that at any moment my toes were going to shoot off my foot like projectiles. I excused myself and pulled another seat up close and lifted my leg up, before it exploded.

"Can I join you?" a soft voice asked, and like a ray of light, Marie appeared at the door.

"Of course," I said, speaking for everyone, and Phillipe's rage returned, and he left the table without anyone suspecting why.

I tried to get up clumsily, to pull a chair out for Marie, but Pete pushed me back where I was. I felt like a fool, and was sure that everyone there knew now that I was keen on her.

Her sheer presence made me feel a range of emotions I'd never felt before. And to some extent, the intensity of the feeling bothered me.

I tried to cover my feelings up, pretending that nothing had happened, but my nervousness gave me away. What was happening, I wondered. I was a master in keeping my true feelings to myself. But here, in her presence, I felt like a boy.

I took a deep breath and fortunately Pete changed the subject, giving me a breather. "Tell us a little about your work, Marie? By the look of it you've got your hands full."

"You're not wrong there," she sighed. "But it's very rewarding seeing animals regain their health and walk free again. The mature animals have passed the rehabilitation phase and are strong enough to look after themselves now. We've released them into different reserves where they're safe from this epidemic. But it's a different story with the smaller animals, like the one you brought here today. There's so many of them. We treat them, vaccinate them and look after them for months or even years before they're released. It's a very slow process. We're like their adopted parents. And they depend on us physically and emotionally. Most of them lost their mothers at the breast-feeding stage and we have to replace them and satisfy all their needs."

"I see, and how do you do that?" I asked, easing my way back into the conversation.

"When they're out of danger," she went on, "and they realize that they're without their mother in a different place to their normal habitat, they become depressed and feel unprotected and that's when we give them as much as we can. It's like they're little orphans. They sleep with us. We give them affection, play with them, give them the milk bottle throughout the day and at night. They even wear nappies."

I was fascinated. "And what happens if one of these adopted parents has to go away during all of this?"

"That's a real problem," she sighed. "Because we can't let the animal suffer another loss like the one they've already had. That's why gradually we start sharing the caring and they become less dependent on the first adopted parent. It seems to work, but some are more sensitive than others. And as a consequence, suffer more."

Her words made me think back to losing contact with Jackie, and wondering whatever happened to my own child. A stab of guilt ran through me with the thought, and I lowered my head, reflecting on my mistakes and the bad decisions that I'd inevitably made during my life.

A few weeks earlier I'd thought differently, but now, after everything that had happened in Gajha, after Thabo's death, Galijha's, the look on the face of the baby baboon dying in my arms, and Marie's words here in the room. They were all like detonators to the bomb I'd been building throughout my whole life.

It was hard to face the fact that I'd lived without true feeling. In a vain, material and fast-moving world that had only served the shell that John Carmichael suddenly appeared to be. I'd stepped outside myself and more than hard, it was shattering to look in the mirror that had suddenly appeared before me. I'd been playing catch-up all my life, satisfying my real needs in a series of interminable compensations that with time had pushed me further and further into an empty, lonely world. I drank some more Konyagi, as if that would help me mitigate the pain, and kept my thoughts to myself, saying nothing, listening to the conversation during dinner.

I felt dizzy, and didn't know if it was because of the liqueur, or the whirlwind of emotions inside of me. So, just before midnight, I excused myself, saying that I was tired and needed to sleep. I got up, put my hands on the table and felt the blood race back to my foot. The pain was unbearable, but I tried not to show my discomfort and left the table. But before I started off, Marie asked me if I needed any help to walk back to the bedroom, and in spite of my condition, the tempting offer made me forget the pain. "Yes, that would be nice," I said.

I was exhausted, but her hand on my arm was like a dive in the ocean and we talked all the way to the bedroom door. I leaned down and kissed her on the cheek, and smiling, she said she'd bring an anti-inflammatory and a pain killer straight back, to help me sleep through the night. Mike was still asleep and without making any noise, or putting the light on, I undressed, thinking only of going to sleep. But Marie, true to her word, came back with the medication she'd promised, and a jar of water. She put it on the side table, and pouring me a glass, whispered: "Take this, John. Now rest and tomorrow I'll come back early and look at the two of you."

I watched her go through the door, feeling confused and depressed. And closing my eyes, the night came to an end. Hours later, after tossing and turning under the sheets, my thoughts became clearer and I could see an answer to some of my doubts. For the first time ever, instead of just taking, I decided, for the simple pleasure of doing it, that I would give.

CHAPTER
FOURTEEN

I woke up better the next morning than I had the previous days. Pete was asleep and Mike was sitting up in bed reading some pages from a green folder on his legs. It was eight o'clock.

"How do you feel, Mike?" I asked him, yawning.

"A bit better, but I don't have any strength in my arm and that's driving me batty!" he said, making a fist, then opening and flexing his hand again.

Pete half-opened his eyes and started to stretch, but didn't look like he'd be getting out of bed soon. We were all doing it hard. "What are you reading?" Pete asked from the far side of the room.

"Someone opened the door a while ago and left this on the chest of drawers," Mike answered, lifting the papers up and waving them in the air. "It's a pro-environmentalist study, with a detailed report on the region. All the information and answers we've been looking for, seem to be here."

"What's it say?" I asked, settling my head back on the pillow.

"It talks about the mission to preserve the wildlife, the flora and the position of the people in the territory who've been affected by the industrial plants located on the banks of Lake Victoria."

He stopped and looked down to the bottom of the page, before continuing. "According to this, Tanzania is 945,000 square kilometres, of which approximately 54,000 are occupied by lakes and lagoons. The largest of which is Lake Victoria, the most important fresh water lake in Africa and the second largest by area in the world. As you know it spills over the border into neighboring countries and has a surface area of 69,482 square kilometres."

"That's one big lake," I said.

Mike nodded, but he had his newsreader's hat on, and seemed to be enjoying himself. "It says that agriculture and fishing are the principal economic activities, but both are currently in decline. And for that reason, other industries besides mining: breweries, textile factories and paper manufacturers, have exceeded the safety limit in polluting the lake."

I looked at Pete, who was frowning. It wasn't exactly good news, first thing in the morning.

Mike took another page out of the folder. "This study shows that the factories, in Tanzania alone, produce an estimated two million tons of industrial waste a day. And on top of that, the mining industry goes through seventy-nine million tons of ore to produce one ounce of gold. And all that filth finishes up in the same place."

"They're talking about Gahja specifically, aren't they?" Peter said.

"Yes," Mike affirmed without taking his eye off the

paper. "The government it would seem doesn't have the guts to face the situation and the mining union has been accused of being implicated in this environmental rape."

"We already know that," I said.

"Yes, I know, but wait," Mike said, continuing to read from the page. "As these companies are acquiring new concession in this region, the poor farmers are losing their right to the land and water. Hundreds of kilometres of forests have disappeared, which directly affects villages in the area, not to mention, the flora and fauna."

Mike put all the sheets of paper that were scattered over the bed back together again. "The ecosystems began to be altered after 'we,' the Europeans, came to this land. The imbalance that the environment suffered then affected different ethnic groups that were subjected to slavery to exploit the region's natural resources. It doesn't matter where, or how far 'we' go from Europe, we always do the same thing. We seem incapable of respecting the greatness and integrity of other cultures."

"I couldn't agree more," I said. "It's the very same instinct of superiority that we're born within our beloved England. It's some sort of genetic information that makes us feel better than everyone else. The one who's got the most, carries the biggest stick. Like the law of the jungle says: the strongest survives and also leads."

"What a pity," Peter said, shrugging his shoulders. "But I'm more interested in the Reserve. Does it say anything important about that?"

"I haven't got that far yet. After breakfast, I'll keep reading through it. What do you reckon?"

"Perfect, I'm starving," I said, getting out of bed and going to the bathroom, when halfway there, I saw Mike look at his watch. "Christ! What's the date?" he said.

"The twenty-eighth," Pete answered straight away.

"It's Ryan's birthday," Mike said, frowning, thinking about his son. "And no damn telephone around to make a call."

"You'd have to go to Shinyanga," Pete suggested.

Mike shook his head, he knew going there wasn't on the agenda. So, he changed tack. "What can I get a fourteen-year-old boy as a present around here?"

"A thirteen-year-old girl," I called out, sticking my head through the bathroom door.

They both laughed.

There were more than a dozen people in the dining room when we got there. But there was no sign of Marie. She'd already eaten, or was working before breakfast. Mike was on the mend, and had come with us, which was a good sign.

"How'd you sleep?" Turner asked, coming over to our table.

"Great," Pete answered.

"Fine, eat well. We'll head off around ten o'clock," he said. "As well as the Reserve we'll take you to some of the villages near the lake."

He walked off, and still starving, I ate a bowl of cereal and fruit, accompanied by a hot cup of tea. But I was too curious to find out how the baby baboon had spent the night, so I passed on second helpings, and left the others at the table.

I bumped into Marie halfway to the clinic pavilion. She was carrying a sleeping monkey in her arms. I kissed her on the cheek, like I'd done the night before, and asked her about the little baboon. "She's still weak," she answered in that soft French accent of hers. "We'll have to wait a few more days to see if her progress is on track."

"I'd like to see her if I could. We're going on that tour of the Reserve soon. And I'd feel better if I saw her before we set off."

She smiled that beautiful smile of hers and said, "Of course." And we walked together into the pavilion.

The little baboon opened its eyes as soon as we walked into the room, and began to squeal. She tried to stand up, but didn't have enough strength yet. I put my hand in the cage and stroked her, and she went perfectly still, waiting for me to pick her up.

"You're her father," Marie said. "You saved her life, and were the first person she saw and smelt after her mother's death. Your smell calms her."

"My smell...?"

"That's right," Marie confirmed. "When she's better, she can spend more time with you."

"But I don't know how long we'll be here. I don't want her to get used to me and then ..."

"We'll see, John," Marie interrupted me. "We'll see what happens."

I didn't know whether to pick her up or not. My old habit of avoiding responsibility was back. I just wanted the little animal to get better. That was all. We had a lot of work ahead of us. And I wasn't going to have much free time, and certainly not time to play the role of adopted father.

I stayed with Marie for a while, talking about other things, and then accompanied her back to the others, who were sitting on the steps at the main entrance.

"You haven't given your little girl a name, John," Marie said, with a grin, looking at the surprise on my face. "I'll give you until tonight to come up with one."

I gave her a nervous smile and walked back to the room to collect a few things before we set out. "My little girl," I said, sitting down on the bed, thinking how insistent Marie was, running a dozen names through my head at the same time.

Immersed in my thoughts, I heard Mike and Pete come through the door, laughing. "What's so funny?" I asked them.

"Well, you are," Pete said.

I supposed they already knew about the "little girl" thing, but found out it was more my interest in Marie that they found funny. They knew my track record well enough. But when I told them that I thought Marie was different to all the others, they just laughed louder. And to make matters worse, Marie suddenly appeared at the door, with a stethoscope around her neck and a doctor's bag in her hand. I guessed, judging by the indifferent expression on her face that she hadn't overheard the conversation through the door that had been left half-open. She'd come to check Mike's shoulder and my foot before we left. Telling Mike to lie down on the bed, and undoing his shirt, she began to put light pressure on his chest, moving her hand higher, until he screamed in pain when she pressed down on his shoulder.

"Sorry, Mike," she said, withdrawing her hand. "But I need to check that there's no infection and that the wound's healing well from the inside as well as on the surface of your skin." She ran her hand over his arm again. Then took a pin out and slightly pricked his left arm, all the way down to his hand without Mike showing any reaction at all.

"Why don't I feel any pain?" he asked her.

"It's likely that the bullet's damaged a nerve. But I can't tell for sure at the moment. We'll have to wait until the inflammation comes down. And that could take several weeks." She took a syringe out and extracted a white liquid from a glass blister. Mike watched her like a hawk, a look of horror on his face. "No, Doctor, please don't. I hate injections. Just give me a pill or something."

Marie just smiled and, ignoring his pleas, asked him to pull his trousers down and stop pretending to be a martyr. "There's no other way to do this. You're still exposed to infection and if that happens, things will only get worse."

Reluctantly, Mike lowered his pants and got it over and done with, while battling to keep our laughter under control, we looked on. "Okay, Mike. Take these pills," she said, handing him a bottle. "Every six hours. They'll bring the pain down and soon you'll be back to normal." She turned her attention to me. "Ok, John, now it's your turn. Sit here," she said, pointing to a chair next to the window. "Take your sock off and let's see how your foot is."

Like an obedient child, I did as I was told. The foot was completely bruised around the instep and the ankle. Marie sat on the bed, and holding my foot in her hands, she rested it on her thigh. She put pressure on both sides, turned it slowly in circles, while Pete and Mike chuckled to themselves, and left us alone in the room.

It was a curious form of meditation, having my foot in her hands, resting on her thigh. I could have stayed in that position forever, but a short while later, she put my foot back on the floor.

"I'll have to give you an injection, too, John," she said, taking another syringe and blister out of her collection.

I played it cool, and didn't repeat Mike's theatrical performance. "You're brave, John," she said, after giving me the injection. "Now we'll have to wait for the cortisone to start working. I'll give you the same tablets as Mike. And please let me know how it's going."

I thanked her, kissing her hand this time. "Thanks, Marie, thanks for everything," I said, looking into her eyes, and for the first time since we'd met, I noticed her blush and lower her head shyly. She put her things in the bag in a hurry and turned round when she reached the door. "We'll see each other later today."

I nodded, and thought after she'd left, that it had been nice to see her other side, the reaction of a woman, and not the hard, impenetrable face of a doctor.

CHAPTER
FIFTEEN

We set out on our tour of the Reserve in a powerful four-wheel drive, Pete and I, accompanying Mummbar and Turner, as Bantu drove us through the hundreds of hectares that comprise Gambala Reserve. The sheer variety of wildlife was amazing and we didn't stop taking photos all the way.

Mike had decided to stay at the camp, his arm was still giving him trouble, and he figured the rough ride that was going to take an hour and a half, wouldn't do him any good. Bantu drove us where the wildlife and surrounding vegetation had remained unchanged for millennia.

It was an uplifting experience passing through such a fantastic landscape, where life in all its extraordinary forms was not only respected but completely protected.

I felt privileged to be a witness to the beauty of this world, the complete opposite of the degradation, power lust and corruption that we'd seen at Gajha.

During the trip, and though we felt to some degree as safe as the animals that lived in the Reserve, we kept a watchful eye over our shoulder. We were here after all to listen first hand to the story of the people in the three small villages near the lake, people who'd been directly affected by the ongoing pollution, and who we hoped would play a key role in our plan of attack against the mine.

It was late afternoon by the time we headed back from our visit, and stopped at the edge of the river that crossed the Reserve and marveled at the dozens of animals who'd come down to sate their thirst in the river at this hour. The deluge dropped by the storm two days before had merely freshened the mud pools, lining the river bed, and failed to fill the river itself that had been all but emptied by the drought season.

Small gazelles and impalas played peacefully at the feet of their mothers, while not far away in the muddy water, or hidden by the abundant grass at the river's edge, hungry crocodiles waited their chance. And where the water was deeper, others, like dark shadows, awaited the coming feast patiently.

The heat, like a muggy weight leaning on us, forced us to seek shelter under the trees back from the water. The pain had returned to my foot, so I washed a pain-killer down with a can of cold beer, while Pete busied himself photographing the surroundings. Turner brought us up to date with the devastating repercussions that the mine and logging companies had had upon the environment.

"All these companies are a problem," Turner explained. "But Gajha is our major concern. Everything's out of control and as you've seen in the last few days, it's getting more complicated all the time." While he drank his beer, he undid a large red handkerchief tied around his neck and wiped the sweat off his forehead. "The different factions within the mine's administration, have become the equivalent of an untouchable mafia. Their tricks are getting darker and more violent day by day, which only makes me believe that there are other interests involved. We're almost sure that they operate in complicity with gangs of drug traffickers or arms smugglers, given that a clandestine landing strip has been discovered a few miles from the mine. An aircraft loaded with hundreds of boxes lands on a weekly basis. Armed guards have been seen supervising the unloading, and two of the mine's directors have been directly involved in the goings on."

"Exactly!" Pete interrupted. "We saw boxes full of guns in the warehouse, where Thabo and Galijha were killed."

Bantu and I nodded.

"It's obvious that the animals that we saw in Sector 38," I said, "are only a part of this puzzle. They kill anyone who happens to stumble in on them, and it's as if they just get swallowed up by the earth itself, and disappear without a trace. They know that one search warrant could bring everything out in the open and bring the whole gold mine crashing down."

"I agree," Mummbar said. "That's all the more reason why we should be careful, because they're not just simple, corrupt mine officials, they're traffickers and killers. The main problem is that we can't act alone, I mean, without the support of the law. But at the same time, we don't know whom to trust and whom not to trust."

"I think the only way out," Turner added, "is to put the whole thing in the hands of international ecological and human rights groups. Presuming that you go ahead with what was planned, and the more proof we have, the more difficult it will be for them to refute it. And the easier it will be to bring them down. They can't be permitted to get away with this forever."

Peter raised his camera. "We've already got plenty and also John photographed the weapons in the boxes."

We stayed there in the shade of the trees talking it over for a long while, and then continued our trip back to camp, but a few miles down the road, the van came to an abrupt halt. Bantu got out and lifted the bonnet up, and a trace of black smoke trailed into the sky. "There's a crack in the radiator."

"Could it have been a branch, Bantu?" Mummbar asked, standing next to him.

"I doubt it. The hole's right here. At the top," he explained, pointing. "I don't see how that could've happened."

While Mummbar and Bantu tried to work out what had happened, Turner took the radio telephone out of the van and after several attempts, confirmed that no one was answering back at the camp.

"It's strange that no one's in the hut or my office. Either Phillipe or Gatto should be there!"

"Who's Gatto?" I asked.

"The guard at the main gate. He sometimes feeds the animals and knows perfectly well that the hut can't be left unattended without asking for back up," Turner said, rubbing his chin. And to make matters worse, we were a long way from camp, too far to walk with the equipment, and much too far for my foot.

"Bantu," Turner said in a firm voice that betrayed a sense of urgency. "Something must have happened to Gatto and Phillipe. It doesn't make any sense that no one's there to answer the phone. Somebody's got to go and get help. We'll wait here, and I'll keep ringing until someone answers. Here, take the rifle."

"Very well, sir. I'll be back as soon as I can," he said, running down the track with surprising speed.

We went back under the trees, while Peter took the camera and said he wanted to take some shots of the river.

"Be careful, Peter. Don't go too far away," Mummbar warned him, sitting down on a folding chair that he'd taken out of the jeep. "It's dangerous, wandering around here with so many wild animals around."

"I won't be long. I'll just take a few photos nearby."

Hours later, Peter still hadn't returned. "I'm going to see if I can find him," I told the others. "He should've been back here a long time ago."

Turner took the remaining rifle out of the vehicle, handed it to me and I walked off in the direction Pete had been heading a few hours before. I called his name as I walked along the track, but there was no answer and no sign of him. I started to think the worst. There were plenty of predators around, and my nerves were starting to get the better of me wondering which one. But right then, as my imagination was working overtime, a shot rang through the silence, frightening a flock of geese to take flight, filling the sky above me completely.

CHAPTER
SIXTEEN

I stopped in my tracks, adrenalin pumping through my veins, running in the direction the shot had come from. The screeching of birds and the shouting of monkeys was pounding my ears. I was running back towards the riverbank, when suddenly I saw Peter, with his back to me, rifle in hand, looking at something thrashing wildly in the water. "What happened, Pete?" I called out running towards him.

But he just shook his head, without taking his eye off the thrashing whirlpool at the edge of the river. "I was filming the spider monkeys," he said, when I got to him, "when a pair of them started to fight over a piece of fruit, chasing each other through the branches. It slipped out of the carrier's hands and the other monkey, the small one, leaned down to pick it out of the water, when a crocodile surfaced and took the whole monkey in one bite."

He continued shaking his head, the horrific sight engraved in his mind. "When I saw that, I just fired without thinking. I guess, I hoped the shot would frighten the croc and he'd let the monkey go. But that was just wishful thinking. His instinct was greater than his fear."

I looked above, the monkeys were screeching hysterically in the trees.

"Just thank your lucky stars that it was the monkey and not you," I said, as Mummbar and Turner ran up to us.

Turner's face was flushed from the effort of running. "Are you all right, Peter? What the hell happened?"

He told the story again, as we walked back to the van, to which Turner replied, putting his hand on Pete's shoulder. "Look, Peter. I know it seems cruel. But it's how it is. It's inevitable. Some have to die, so others can live. It's life's delicate balance. If it were any other way nature itself, would be thrown into chaos."

"I understand that, but it's impossible to see a thing like that and rationalize it and just say it's part of the big picture," Pete explained. "I just reacted instinctively; mammal against reptile."

Turner smiled. "But when everything's said and done, the big picture, as you describe it, is how it ultimately is!"

We all lifted our heads and looked down the road as another 4-wheel drive came hurtling towards us with Marie and Bantu inside.

"What happened?" Turner asked Marie as she got out. "Why hasn't anyone answered the phone back at camp?"

"I don't know," she answered. "I saw Gatto this morning, but I haven't seen Phillipe all day."

Turner bit his lip and took a deep breath, while Bantu got to work fixing the radiator, and thirty minutes later we drove back to camp.

Mike was standing at the front of the main pavilion

with a concerned look on his face. "We were all worried about you, men."

"Everything's all right now," I told him. "We had a problem with the van," I said, my attention distracted by a tall African with a rifle in his hand walking towards us.

"Gatto," Turner called to him, a few yards away. "Why didn't you answer the radio phone?"

"The transmitter cables were cut. It must have been deliberate," he said, as he arrived at the group. "I've been trying to fix it all day."

"And where were you?" Turner asked Phillipe who'd been following Gatto.

"I've been in Shinyanga the whole day, restocking food and medication. I only found out that something had gone wrong when I got back."

"I think the radiator was tampered with," Bantu said, cutting in. "It was in perfect condition earlier this morning."

It seemed like more than just coincidence that the radiator and the transmitter had both malfunctioned at the same time, and the thought threw an air of uncertainty and suspicion into the group.

Turner clenched his fists and staring at us, said, "I'm afraid, my friends, this is getting too dangerous around here for you to stay on. You're my responsibility and we brought you here to help. But…"

I interrupted him. "We can't just run off with our tails between our legs. That would be just playing into their hands."

"We have to stop this outrage," Marie said angrily. "We've got to advise the police before it's too late. With no disrespect to those present, these Englishmen, McMahon and Dormonth, only came here to cause trouble and corrupt people. I'm sure they're the ones behind all of this, and they've put the others up to it for a few miserable shillings. They've got a small army working for them, doing whatever they want. And nothing gets back to them. They think that we'll be scared off. But I won't be."

"Marie's right," Mummbar said, looking at Turner. "Even though we can't trust the police, and it's very likely they're collaborating with UMAG and the politicians. We still have to see this through to the end, whatever the consequences."

"Listen!" Turner said to Mummbar and Marie. "What you're saying is true. Nobody can argue with that. But you can't involve innocent people in all of this."

Turner stopped talking and looked at us with a look of resignation on his face. He knew we weren't going to give up easily. "If you're willing to go ahead with this, so be it. But if you decide to drop out, I'll understand your decision perfectly."

We looked at each other in silence. It wasn't the same for the three of us. Peter was about to be a father for the first time and Mike had two young sons and a sick wife. But I, on the other hand, had nothing to lose.

"We're a team," Pete said. "But the circumstances in which we find ourselves throws a slant on that, and nobody can be forced to stay on. It's become personal now, and very dangerous. So for me, from this moment on, everyone's free to make his own mind up."

It seemed like the right time to stand up and be counted. "As far as I'm concerned, I don't have anything better to do. It's not just a question of the time and money invested. It's about putting things right. I wouldn't feel right walking out now. For you two, it's completely different. You've got families and responsibilities. But that's not my case. And I don't like the idea that the people we've seen die here have given their life up for nothing. We're very close to having enough film to put these bastards away. And I don't want to see us put a lid on what we've already got and file it away in some drawer somewhere."

"Nobody's going to do that," Mike objected. "As you just said, we've almost got enough for a good documentary. But on a personal level, I've got to think it over carefully. Sarah and the family have to come first."

Pete joined in. "I understand you perfectly. I'm more or less in the same situation. John's already made his mind up. But like you said before, we need time to think. And while that sounds fair enough, there isn't any damn time to think. So, I'm going to throw my hat in with John. I got us all into this in the first place. And he's right. We owe Galijha and Thabo something."

"We're going to beef up security," Turner interrupted. "Put a twenty-four hour guard on the camp. And we've got others on our side. And with their help, it should be enough. But I warn you before we go any further, we can't be sure we'll be successful. There aren't any guarantees."

"Ok, ok," Mike grumbled. "The warrior, even if he's afraid, never leaves the battle field."

"Mike, take your time," I said. "It's not your battle. Do what your heart tells you and don't let what we do pressure you. Even if you go back now, you'll still be in, on the last stage of the project."

"I know, I know. Give me till tomorrow to think it over."

Phillipe who'd been quiet during the conversation, excused himself, saying he wanted to rest. And Turner invited us to his quarters where there were two sofas on an old mud floor and several chairs around an unused chimney. All the tension had left us by the time we sat down and Mummbar offered us a rose wine from the region of Tanzania where his wife came from. He relaxed after the first drink, made a toast and wished us success in whatever we did in the next few days. An hour later, Marie entered with the little baby baboon clinging to her chest. I stood up immediately, and she walked over to me and held the little animal out to me, saying: "Here is your little girl, John. She's getting better, and now she needs her father. You'll have to sleep with her, so she doesn't feel so lonely. And feed her when she wakes up during the night."

"No way!" I said, surprised. "Is this a joke?"

"No, John. It's no joke. I'll help you during the day. But you're on your own at night," she said, raising her eyebrows, amused. "There's no need to be scared. I'll tell you what to do. If she's warm and she's eaten well, she'll sleep like the baby she really is."

"Exactly," Pete said, laughing. "Babies wake up every three hours to eat."

"Don't be too cocky, Pete," Mike warned him. "In a few months you'll be going through all of this, too. Thank God all of that's behind me."

Marie held the little baboon in the air in front of me. "Take her, John. It's no joke."

There was obviously no way out, so I took the tiny animal, cradled her on my chest and walked to the sofa. Staring at the little ball in my arms, at her peaceful face, which made me smile, I said, "Nina" stroking her little head. "I'll call you Nina Carmichael."

"You look like her real father," Pete called across the room. And everyone laughed.

Suddenly the door opened and Bantu came running in. "Mister Turner, Mister Turner," he said, excitedly. "I've just spoken to Gatto and an informant from the mine's told him that at midnight, a plane will land on their secret landing strip. Government officials are coming to talk to the top brass at the mine. It's all about business."

"What are you talking about, Bantu?" Turner asked, standing up.

"I'm telling you exactly what Gatto told me. There's some sort of deal going on."

"Very interesting," Turner said, sitting down again, glancing thoughtfully at Mummbar.

"What are you thinking of doing?" I asked Turner.

After looking around the room for a while, he said seriously: "Tell Gatto to come here straight away. You can mind his post for a while." Looking at his watch, he told Bantu: "When he goes back to the hut, you'll drive Peter, John and me there. Gatto can stay here. No one knows the country as well as you do. Mummbar will stay here with Mike."

Bantu disappeared and a few minutes later, Gatto, a seven-foot-tall Masai, appeared at the door. He repeated what Bantu had just told us.

Turner questioned him for a long while and decided that we could take advantage of the situation and get more conclusive proof about what was happening at the mine. He outlined what he had in mind to the rest of us, and we all got up to go, except Mike and Marie who were going to stay behind. But little Nina didn't seem too pleased to be separated from me, which made me smile. I felt a sudden burst of pleasure in being needed so much by this little animal. It was difficult to describe a sensation that I'd never felt in my life before.

I passed her into Marie's arms and kissed the doctor on the cheek. She smiled softly, as I patted Nina again on her little head and left.

Bantu was behind the wheel of the 4-wheel drive outside, and we all jumped in, but Turner told Gatto to stay behind. "We need the camp guarded, Gatto. There's no point all of us going to Gajha."

The Masai went back to his post.

During the drive there, Turner told Bantu to cut the high beam and take the short cut along a track that was almost never used. Minutes later, driving slowly through the swamp zone, the van got bogged in a deep ditch and came to a complete stop. Everybody cursed at the same time, as Bantu put the vehicle into reverse, then into drive, but the van hardly moved, the smell of burnt rubber filling the air.

Bantu turned the motor off. "Everybody out," he sighed. "See if you can find a big rock or something on the track to put under the tire."

We wandered around like blind men in the dark, until Peter came back with a large flat rock, which he set in the hole under the wheel. "Give it another go now, Bantu," Pete called out, as we all leaned into the back of the van and pushed as hard as we could. And after a couple of failed attempts, the vehicle roared free.

"We could've done without that," Turner said, as we continued on through low scrub, towards the airfield that wasn't too far away.

Bantu cut the lights and we drove up slowly, using the landing strip lights as a guide through the otherwise impenetrable darkness, finally coming to a stop behind some low dunes, thirty yards from the runway. I looked at my watch. It was twenty minutes to midnight.

Pete and I took our equipment out, and I explained to Turner that the high resolution lenses would work without the need of a flash. And taking up our positions, in the bush well behind the dunes, we heard the whirr of propellers in the distance, and saw a file of cars driving along the edge of the landing strip. They pulled up under an intermittent red reflector that directed its light onto the runway.

A dozen men got out of the vehicles and Pete and I started filming the plane's arrival, as it landed and taxied over to the others. The door opened and three men came down the steps, one of them dressed in a dark suit, carrying a folder under his arm. The other two had rifles slung over their shoulders. The suited man walked towards the group on the tarmac, speaking to two men who came forward from the rest: one in a white shirt, the other wearing a red jacket with yellow trim, carrying a metal briefcase. They met in the middle of the tarmac, ten yards from the plane.

"I think the bloke in the white shirt's Dormonth," Pete whispered, observing him through the camera.

We all heard him, but said nothing.

There seemed to be some sort of disagreement going on among those on the landing strip. The man in the white shirt, possibly Dormonth, was waving his hands in the air, apparently annoyed with the man from the plane. They argued for a few minutes more until the man carrying the briefcase opened it, my lens zooming in on its contents: a briefcase full of bundles of notes. The man in the suit flicked carefully through the money, before he handed the folder over, and just as he did, Peter inexplicably cried out.

Everything had gone well for us until that moment, but after hearing Peter's scream, the powerful lights of a reflector from the landing strip tower focused directly on us, thrusting us suddenly out from our hiding place to centre stage.

We took one quick look at each other, grabbed the equipment and sprinted for the van, as something exploded behind.

I got there, hobbling, a little behind the others, and jumped in after them, as Bantu threw the van into first, and put his foot to the board, shots hitting the ground all around us.

As soon as we'd driven far enough away to think

that we'd made good our escape, Turner turned his attention to Peter. "Why did you do that, Peter? You gave us away. And now these bastards won't let up until they catch us."

Pete's jaw dropped and still panting from the effort of running, he said in a weak voice: "A spider bit me!" before he vomited through the window, and his head flopped against the door.

"Did you see the spider?" Bantu asked, speeding through the scrub. "See what colour it was?"

"Reddish, I think. But it all happened so quickly and it was dark. It was big though," he said leaning his head out the window again.

Seeing the condition Peter was in, Turner urged Bantu to tell us what he knew about spiders. "Sounds like a Red Trap Door. You find them everywhere around here. They're very aggressive and poisonous. But not deadly."

"As soon as we get back we'll get Marie to give him something. But by the sound of it he'll be sick for days," Turner grumbled, still worried about the consequences of what had just happened.

When we got to the intersection that we'd turned off less than an hour before, we saw a trail of lights heading our way, so Bantu cut the lights and slipped off the main track and onto another that would take us back to the Reserve.

"They're coming after us, sir. What do you want me to do?" Bantu asked nervously, clicking his lips, without taking his eyes off the track ahead.

"Drive slowly and make the least noise possible," Turner said. "And if the lights get close, drive into the bushes, and cut the motor. But they're still a fair way behind us now. I can only hope they didn't identify us."

I looked at Peter, who was grumbling in silence next to me, shaking his head, and keeping his thoughts to himself. Chance hadn't been kind to us back there, and I was as worried as Turner was, about what would happen now.

The drive back to Gambala in the dark seemed to take an eternity, crossing streams, dodging rocks and one dead animal after another. And when we did finally get back, Gatto pushed his lantern up to the window, illuminating our faces, as Turner wound the window down. "Double the security on the gate tonight. There could be trouble heading our way!"

Another guard came out and raised the bar as we drove through the grille, while I watched it close behind us as we made for the pavilion.

We helped Pete back to our dorm. He was still nauseous and breathing with difficulty. I helped him get undressed, and put him into the bed, and in the process, woke Mike up. "What happened to him?" he asked, staring at Pete.

I told him the story, and had just got to the part about our getaway in a hail of bullets, when Marie came in with her travelling doctor's case. "You go and look after Nina," she said to me. "I'll take care of Peter."

I looked down at Pete, who seemed to be in the middle of some great internal battle, and realized there wasn't anything I could do for him. I could only hope, with Marie's care, that he'd recover as soon as possible.

Nina was curled up in bed, a check blue and pink flannel blanket covering her up to the shoulders. I closed the door, took my jacket off and lay down beside the baby baboon, stroking her little head, running my eyes over each of her features. She half opened her eyes and stretched her little hands out to touch my chest, as I passed my hand over her tiny body and let it rest on her back, pulling her closer to me. She took my index finger and put it in her mouth, sucking softly, emitting almost imperceptible grunts, as she slipped back to sleep. I closed my eyes, and a while later fell asleep at her side.

Hours later, with my eyes closed, I could hear Nina grunting as she put her warm palm on my face, playing with the tip of my nose. Opening my eyes, and lifting my head, I could see that Marie was fast asleep on the other side of the bed. I leaned across and softly woke her up. She looked at the alarm clock, and yawning, took the milk bottle and a white cloth that was on the side table next to her, and handed them over to me without saying a word. I settled back in the bed, leaning on the bed head, watching Nina wide awake, following the delicious white liquid in the bottle in my hand. I sat her on my thighs and clumsily put the teat in her mouth, as she grabbed the bottle in her hands and drank desperately, a thread of milk trailing out of her mouth, and falling onto her wet chest.

Marie, who was watching the whole scene in silence, reached out and pointed to the cloth that lay folded on the bed. "Put it under her chin, John. She's getting wet."

"I wasn't exactly born for this." I said nervously, without taking my eye off Nina. It's hard work."

Marie smiled and stretched her hand out and stroked Nina's little head. "Don't worry too much, John. She's only a baby."

I turned away from the tiny baboon and looked into Marie's blue eyes, as my pulse began to race. I looked back at Nina immediately. Marie noticed that, and shyly looked at the light of the lamp outside the window.

"Be careful, John," she whispered.

"What are you talking about, Marie?" I asked looking back at her.

"I'm afraid something might happen to you. These men around here are as cold as they come. You should leave as soon as possible," she said, staring at me, from across the bed.

I reached across and stroked her hair that lay like a golden mantle on the pillow. "We can't stop now. It's gone too far for that. Somebody has to make a stand. We'd be cowards to give up now," I said staring into her eyes. "It's the first time in my life that I've felt like this. I'm prepared to go all the way."

"But John," she protested. "What are you going to achieve if you're dead? What if it comes to that? Is it worth dying for?"

"We're here," I said, lowering my voice. "We've got plenty of material already. And I'm sure it's going to help stop this land being destroyed. Someone's got to do it."

I looked back at Nina, who was watching my every move, as she continued to suck from the bottle. I pulled my hand back from Marie and stroked Nina's little face; she shuddered and closed her eyes almost immediately, fast asleep, as more milk dripped out of her mouth.

I knew in that moment why Marie had fallen in love with Africa.

Marie fell silent for a few moments, until I decided to ask her a few questions about her life, to which she responded with a faraway look in her eyes. "I was born in the French provinces, in a small town called Vaucluse. I lived there with my parents and three older brothers. Our house was in the middle of a field of lavender, a business that our family had been involved in for generations. We also produced truffles," she said smiling, closing her eyes and remembering their taste. "I lived my whole childhood there, in those purple fields that smelt like... home."

I was intrigued. "Then, why did you leave France and come to live in a place like Africa?"

"Because I always loved animals. I studied in Paris to be a veterinary-zoologist and finished up specializing in primates. After completing my university studies, the opportunity came up to travel to Tanzania for a few months with a group of specialists, to try and help the Papio Reserve come out of one of the worst crises in its history."

"And Phillipe? I suppose he was one of the group, wasn't he?" I asked her, testing the water.

"Yes," she said. "Why do you ask?"

"No reason in particular. But he doesn't seem too pleased when I'm around you."

She grinned, shaking her head. "No, it's not like that. Phillipe is only a good friend. He's married and has a family in Belgium. He knows well enough that our relationship is only professional," she said, without giving it any more thought.

"And getting back to Papio, at that time, there were a lot of chimpanzees in the Reserve, and an epidemic of simian smallpox had broken out. The situation was complicated by a virus that affected the hearts of many of the chimps. A third of the population died, and I finished up taking over the administration of the Reserve after we got it back on its feet. I came to Gambala after that, for reasons that you know only too well."

"And you've never thought of returning to France? You give me the impression that you've settled down here."

"I've been back for short visits. But..." she reached out and took Nina's hand tenderly. "This is my home now. It fills me with life more than I could ever have imagined. I know that it seems strange to others, but everyone has a vocation, and I've found mine here." I looked at her for a while, then slowly took her hand and kissed it. She looked away, and the silence was impenetrable, until suddenly, Nina broke it, finishing the bottle and lying on my legs.

Marie picked her up and slid off the bed, changed her nappy and then put her in a wooden drawer, where she covered her with the flannel blanket, as she fell asleep in front of our eyes. Marie came back to the bed. My first reaction was to leave and go back to my room, but something stopped me doing that. I didn't want that moment to end. I wanted time to stop. I wanted to stay there forever.

I lay down beside her, felt her body next to mine, put my arm around her, her head resting on my chest. This was what I'd wanted from the first moment I'd seen her. But it was more than that now. My heart beating wildly as I lifted her head to mine.

It was more than a kiss, more than magic. It was an explosion, a mad charge of desire unlocked. A storm!

She undid the buttons on my shirt, kissed my chest and each garment was tossed aside. The deeper we moved into this strange new world, the more my heart opened, the further the ghosts of the past, the fear of commitment, receded.

Nina woke up early in the morning, and terrified, began to cry, crouching in a corner of her wooden drawer. I jumped up, and Marie turned the side-table lamp on, its weak light revealing Nina screaming out of control, waving her little hands desperately in the air.

"What's wrong with her?" I asked, taking the blanket off her, as Marie lifted her up.

"I don't know, John," Marie said, running her hand over Nina's body, as I checked the mattress for any signs of an insect.

Nina was still scared, twisting in Marie's arms, stretching her hands out towards me. I took her from Marie and tried to calm her down, gave her the milk bottle, but nothing worked. Nothing made what had frightened her, go away.

CHAPTER
SEVENTEEN

After the hectic night before, the sun began to rise. I got out of bed and looked through the window at its first rays painting the sky pink and violet. Spongy clouds stretched for miles in every direction, and on the outskirts of the camp, a pair of impalas roamed around, watching the movement of workers doing the rounds of the adult baboon cages. Nina had finally calmed down after several hours of restlessness and was now resting on Marie. She hadn't taken her little round eyes off me for a second, as if she was afraid I would disappear.

I was beginning to worry about the tie that was being built between us; I didn't want to see the poor little animal go through another loss like she already had with her mother.

"I can't do this, Marie," I said, holding Nina's hand, looking at her tenderly. "The more time I spend with her the worse it will be when we have to separate. You know I've got to return to London. It doesn't seem fair."

Marie looked away, keeping her thoughts to herself. Then she sighed and tried to smile. "I'll miss you, too, Johnny. But I know that's how life is," she said, calling me Johnny, just like my grandmother had done, all those years before. "We belong to different worlds, John."

"I'll come back for you, Darling. Don't worry about that," I said, kissing her softly on the forehead. "For the first time in my life, I've found something that's bigger than me. It's as though I can suddenly feel and share for the first time. There's no way I'll let that go."

"If you ever come back to Tanzania, John, it will be to live here, because I'll never leave Africa. This is my home. I'll live and die here," she said, staring into my eyes. "I hope you will come back. I'll be waiting for you."

It was more than clear to me at that moment, that I'd fallen completely in love with her, and that it was already going to be difficult to leave.

We got dressed and left the room at eight o'clock, with Nina in my arms, heading for the pavilion. But halfway there, we came across a commotion in front of one of the cages. Women were crying, their hands over their faces, horrified.

"What happened?" Marie asked, running ahead.

"Gatto's dead," Bantu said, with his head in his hands.

"He can't be," Marie protested. "But how? How did he die?"

"We don't know, Doctor. It looks like it happened around dawn."

"There was a blow to his head," another man said, examining Gatto's body inside the cage.

For five years he'd been doing the same thing every morning, and now there he was, dead on the floor of the cage, observed by a huddle of baboons in a corner.

As far as I could make out, it was the first time in the history of the park that one of the workers had died. I walked up to Turner, who was surrounded by Peter, Mike and Mummbar, and they all seemed as shocked as everyone else.

"It doesn't strike me as being an accident," Turner said. "Baboons don't attack someone who's feeding them."

It occurred to me then that Gatto's death had something to do with what had happened the night before. And judging by the expressions on Turner and Mummbar's faces, it seemed they thought the same. Marie entered the cage and examined Gatto carefully.

"There's a wound in the stomach," she observed. "It seems he was stabbed first and hit on the head afterwards."

All activity at the Reserve came to a halt that morning. The suspicion that there was a killer amongst us had everyone looking over their shoulders. Turner tried to calm the workers down, saying it was something the authorities would have to solve. But his words fell on deaf ears, and I had the impression that many there blamed Peter, Mike and me for what had happened.

Our visit to the Reserve hadn't been well explained, and given the circumstances, and the fact that nothing like this had happened before our arrival, our presence there now was viewed with suspicion.

After a few hours, and still in the middle of the chaos, I asked Pete if he still felt the effects of the spider's bite. "It's burning like hell," he said. "And I'm dizzy. But apart from that I'm still alive."

And being alive counted for a lot right then, as a squad of police arrived on the scene to conduct an investigation. They interviewed everyone, us included, and all we could tell them was that we were English and were on a photographic safari, and that we had come to Gambala on the invitation of Mummbar and Turner.

They wrote that down along with pages of notes from all the other interviews, convinced that the killer had to be one of those residents at Gambala. While the interviews were being conducted, Marie's assistants fed the animals, because the rest of the workers had gone on strike. The women worked overtime, carrying saucepans full of fruit, among other things, to the larger animals, and bottles of milk to the smaller ones. All of which Peter and I filmed, along with the rest of the frenetic activity.

Mike helped out, too. He seemed to be almost back to normal, a week after having been shot. And the possibility of him having to explain why he'd been shot had already crossed our minds. We couldn't say that it had been a stray bullet, or confess that he'd been shot at Gajha. There didn't seem any readymade answer at all, if it came to him actually being asked. And when it was his turn to be questioned, I stood nearby, pretending to wind a camera tape. At that very moment, Phillipe walked up to me and said in a bitter voice, "Ever since you arrived, things have been falling apart. Turner and Mummbar made a big mistake in inviting you here. You've only brought trouble with you. And keep away from Marie."

"What's that supposed to mean?" I said, lifting my head from the camera and staring at him. "That's none of your business!"

He just raised his eyebrows and shrugged his shoulders, without saying anything else, then left me fuming, wanting to ram my fist into his face.

Immediately after police frisked everyone and double-checked the quarters, the sound of a scream came from our bedroom. Seconds later, a policeman came running out of the corridor, carrying a blood-smeared knife in his handkerchief. "Who sleeps in this section?" he demanded to know.

It was more than obvious in those first few seconds, that someone had planted the knife in our room, with the express intention of involving us in Gatto's murder. Without us even answering, he ordered the three of us along with Turner and Mummbar, to identify whose pillow the knife had been hidden under.

While that was going on, Phillipe stood a few steps behind, shaking his head, as if what he'd said a few minutes before had just been proven right.

We followed the policeman to the room and stared in disbelief as he pointed to one of the unmade beds. "Listen, sir," Peter said, shocked at the whole situation and the fact that his bed was being pointed at. "All of this is absurd. We were all with Gatto last night before he left us. I had no idea where he went. Besides that, what possible motive could I have to kill him? We're traveling through here. We're tourists!" he said, his voice getting angrier all the time.

"Be quiet!" one of the officials said.

Pete looked at us. "I've been set up."

"What are you suggesting?" the official asked. "Are you accusing me of being a liar? You obviously don't know who you are talking to. So, take my advice, my friend, and choose your words very carefully. Because I can see that you're trying to divert attention away from the crime you've committed."

"But… this is ridiculous," Pete protested, as another official cuffed him, and started to lead him to the car they'd arrived in.

Turner came to his defence immediately, repeating in effect, what Peter had just said. Confirming that Gatto hadn't told anyone where he was going and that Peter and Mike had remained behind in their room. But the official would have none of it, saying he was only interested in the facts. And watching the goings on, I had a hunch that there was no way he could be dissuaded.

Mike got involved then, standing in their way in the corridor, putting his hand up. "This is arbitrary," he said. "This is all one big mistake."

"I'm sorry, but the law is the law," the official said, without looking at him. "We'll take him to the police chief in Shinyanga and I suppose being a foreigner, he'll be taken in the next few days to Dodoma or Dar es Salaam. I'm still not sure."

We followed them down the corridor protesting, but it was obvious that the official was a key part of the whole conspiracy. We watched them put Pete in the back seat of the car and I called after him as they drove off. "Don't worry mate. We'll get you out."

It had all happened so fast that it didn't seem real. A few hours before, I'd been on top of the world. But now Gatto had been killed, not far from where Marie and I spent the night together, and Peter was now under arrest for his murder, and on his way to Shinyanga.

Bantu had been watching the events in the distance. Turner called him over. "What happened, sir?"

"They've taken Peter to Shinyanga. Go there and check that he's at the police station and under arrest like this official said."

"Yes, sir," Bantu said, running off, while Turner called the rest of us together in the pavilion, where we spent what was left of the afternoon, trying to decide what our next step should be.

Later, while we were still going over our plans, a villager arrived at four in the afternoon to inform us that Peter had never arrived in Shinyanga.

CHAPTER
EIGHTEEN

Turner got up immediately and walked around the compound like a caged lion, thinking everything over. If they hadn't taken Peter to Shinyanga, then the only other place they could have taken him to was directly to Dodoma, where UMAG had more sway with the local police.

I had the sudden feeling that if we didn't act right away, it would more than likely be too late.

Without giving it another thought, I asked Turner to drive me to the capital to try and find out where Peter was. Mike wanted to come, too, but I ruled that out straight away. " You're not strong enough yet."

Despite what I just said, he insisted, keeping at me for what seemed like ages. However, I kept emphasizing the fact that it wasn't worth the risk, that it was a one man job, given the circumstances.

"Let it be," I told him. "You still haven't recovered from the last incident, without putting your life on the line in this. And I don't fancy carrying any more bad news back to England."

He eventually relented. "You should've been a lawyer, not a photographer."

"Maybe," I admitted, shrugging my shoulders. "But in this situation, I'm only being reasonable."

Turner, after listening to my plan eventually agreed, and made the light aircraft available for the next day, his only son Roger, to travel with me and the pilot.

Roger lived in Mwanza, a couple of hours away, and judging by Turner's description was an ideal choice to go with me to the capital. Besides being a lawyer, he also exported ginger and pepper to Europe, and had plenty of experience in dealing with the locals.

Turner rang him immediately, and after several attempts at trying to get through on the transmitter, a hoarse voice recognized Turner. "What's up, Dad?"

Turner told him what had happened, but as Mike and I were listening to the conversation, it became more than obvious that the father-son relationship had been put to the test before. It seemed that Roger had no interest whatsoever of helping out. But Turner kept at him, explaining the reason for our coming to Tanzania and the help we'd already given him and Mummbar. "And beyond all of that," Turner added. "An innocent man's life's at stake."

"Very well, then. I'll be there tonight," he finally said turning the radio off, without saying goodbye.

Turner breathed a sigh of relief. He'd managed somehow to get his son to accompany me to Dodoma. And at that moment, with nothing else to be grateful for, it seemed a lot.

"I'm sorry you had to listen to a conversation like that," Turner apologized. "But things haven't been good between us for a long time."

"Don't worry," I said. "There are problems in every family."

He feigned a half-smile and said: "And now the pilot."

He picked up the transmitter again, adjusted the frequency, and after several attempts, a distant voice came over the line, between intermittent noise and irritating disturbance. Turner proceeded to explain the situation to the pilot, advising him that we needed the plane at dawn the next morning. But the pilot seemed to have problems of his own, something to do with the landing gear.

"Do whatever you have to, to be here at dawn," Turner shouted into the transmitter.

"The only way is in a Cessna 177," Jamal, the pilot, explained to him. "But it's only good for local flights. I'm not sure it'll make it to either of the two big cities."

"Just get it as ready as you can," Turner snapped.

Unable to dissuade him, Jamal eventually gave in, and said he'd arrive before nine in the morning.

Turner turned the transmitter off and leaned his fists on the table. "Everything's just got too complicated," he despaired. "I can only hope that you and Roger will get there in time to save Peter. The longer he's there, the more chance there is that something terrible will happen."

Mike and I looked at each other. There was no need to say anything. We both knew that Turner was right.

Hours later, when we were at the table picking at our dinner, a tall, fair, stockily-built, ruddy-faced man came through the door. He was carrying a briefcase in his hand, and Turner jumped up to greet him. "This is Roger, my son," he said, introducing him to Marie, Mike and myself, and pulling a chair out at the table for him to join us.

I had no way of knowing what had happened

between the two men, and while I was curious, the urgent situation we were in precluded any speculation about the real reason for the obvious rift between the two men.

I explained the real reason for our trip to Tanzania and told Roger what had happened at Gajha.

He listened attentively to what I had to say and then advised us that the best thing was to go straight to the British Embassy, expose what we'd already seen and establish exactly where Peter had been taken.

He told us that there had been some serious delays in the hearing of cases, and that prison and custodial conditions were very hard in Africa. "It could take days or weeks to find out exactly where Peter is. And if these officials are in collusion with UMAG, as would seem to be likely, listening to what you've already told me, it's going to be very difficult to get him out of there." He shrugged his shoulders and sighed. "I don't want to be a fatalist. But this local mafia will make it next to impossible for you to find any proof in Peter's favour. Either way I don't want to get ahead of myself. Let's put it in the hands of the embassy. They'll have to find a way through all of this."

Turner's son had painted a grim picture of how things worked in Tanzania, and my mood which was already low, hit rock bottom.

There was a lot to be done the next day, so we left the table and headed back to the pavilion. Mike walked quickly ahead, leaving me behind with Marie. "I'd like to see Nina before I go to bed," I told her.

Nina was asleep in the cage, on top of the table, near the window, but on hearing my voice, she opened her eyes, and sat up clumsily and began to squeal, leaning her wrinkled snout against the metal bars.

I smiled, and took her out of the cage, and with her

hands grasping my wrists, I sat down on the edge of the bed.

On any other evening, it would have been another beautiful moment in another long day of discovery. Marie and I together on her bed, Nina clinging to my chest - but it was far from that. Ever since we'd walked out of the room at the beginning of the day, everything had just got progressively worse.

"I'm afraid this could have a terrible ending," Marie confessed, sitting down beside me, putting her hand on my back.

"I know," I said. "The worst thing is that we came here with the idea of helping and we finish up in a situation like this, a set up. It's not only difficult to believe. It's unbearable."

Marie leaned her cheek on my shoulder and, stroking Nina's back, she added, "Just the thought of you going to Dodoma or wherever, frightens me. I can't stand thinking of you dealing with these people."

I kissed her on the forehead tenderly, my hand behind her neck. "It'll be all right."

"I don't know. I don't know what to think," she said, her voice shaking. "I'm afraid if you corner them, they'll kill you. That's what scares me the most. And poor Peter, I just hope you can get him out of there quickly."

"So do I, Marie. But to tell you the truth, I'm worried they're going to hurt him."

"Don't think about that now, Johnny. We've got to be positive and hope that you and Roger can get there on time to stop anything happening."

I fell back on the bed, watching Nina clinging to my shirt with both hands, dragging herself over my ribs, climbing towards my face. The squeal of a gecko, a small phosphorescent green lizard, attracted my attention, as it edged across the moth-bitten ceiling stealthfully, crossing great black leak marks made during the rainy season. Its world, and its precise and slow movement, pulled me away for a few moments from the turbulence of my thoughts.

After nearly an hour with Marie, and after having given Nina her milk, I decided I had to go, but she wanted to hear more about my past. About a life that at that moment seemed so far away.

I told her about my work, my hobbies, and about old Morris, the cat. But I avoided the personal details of my youth that made me feel so uncomfortable.

"And were you ever married, John? Do you have any children?"

I coughed nervously; the last thing I was going to talk about then was Jackie Guirmand. What would Marie think about that? About my cowardice in walking away from the relationship, and the baby Jackie had been expecting. There was no way I could answer the question directly, so I said: "No, I've never been married. But I've had my fair share of relationships and all I can tell you is that it has been difficult for me to make a commitment."

I breathed out, a little wary of listening to any more of my own words. "Unfortunately, my childhood was difficult and I never really had a role model to follow. And it's only now, that all of that has suddenly become much clearer to me."

"I'm sorry, John. Let's leave it there," she said, reaching out and pulling me back to her. "Stay with me tonight."

CHAPTER
NINETEEN

A little before eight the next morning, we all met in front of the van that would take Roger and I to the airfield. Mike gave me Pete's passport and slapped me on the back and said, "Everything will work out. I'm sure of that. Peter's waiting for you."

I wasn't sure if he was right or not, and I guess my expression showed that well enough. I said goodbye to him and the rest, and kissed Marie on the lips, to the surprise of everyone there.

Roger was in the front seat, scribbling in a notebook, so I jumped in the back and closed the door behind me. It took Bantu a while to start the engine, but a few seconds after he did, we were off, leaving a trail of dust in our wake, as Marie's voice carried on the early morning breeze. "Be very careful, John."

We drove in silence and a half an hour later arrived at the airfield that we'd landed at nearly a week before.

"I've got to give the pilot a message from Turner before you take off," Bantu said, quickly past us, towards a man in a neon-yellow t-shirt, which had that many holes in it that it was hard to make out the pattern of love and peace symbols amongst the black moons of the pilot's flesh underneath.

We kept up with Bantu walking towards the red Cessna 177 with the white roof, where we found another man on his back looking up at the fuselage.

He got up straight away, telling us that it was ready for takeoff and went over to the pilot whose back was turned to us and wished him a safe trip.

Jamal nodded, turned around and took our baggage from us, put it in the back of the plane and opened the door for us to get in.

Roger sat in the front, next to the pilot, and spoke for the first time in almost an hour. "I don't have a good feeling about all of this. I only hope the flight will be worth the effort."

"Do you think something's happened to Peter?" I asked.

"I hope not, John. But with these people you never know. There's a great abuse of power here in Tanzania. And things happen."

"So they could kill him then," I said getting to the point.

He nodded. "I'm afraid that's more than possible. A little more than a year ago, a group of Italians arrived here on what was a real photographic safari. They'd travelled from the Serengeti, passed through Ngorongoro, on route to Gajha. They had no idea what was going on here. They were in Africa, looking to have a good time. A little bit of action. That sort of stuff," he paused looking through the window, collecting his thoughts.

"And what happened?" I asked.

"They were found dead on the outskirts of Shinyanga. The only thing that was made public was that cocaine was found in their possession. It was passed off as some sort of dispute between traffickers. And their bodies were sent back to Italy."

"And they'd done nothing?" I asked incredulously.

"More or less. They trod on a few toes. Asked one question too many."

"Put the safety belts on," Jamal told us, pointing to a pair of rusty buckles, as he put his headphones on, and adjusted several buttons and levers on the instrument panel. The plane taxied onto the tarmac, the roar of the motor making conversation difficult. He straightened the Cessna, increased speed, and seconds later we took off, barely making it over a stand of acacia trees at the other end of the runway.

Looking down, I saw a man in a red jacket with yellow trim. The same jacket as the man had been wearing at Gajha landing strip at midnight two nights before. "Jamal! Jamal!" I called out. "Who's that down there?"

The pilot followed my pointing finger back to the airfield. "That's Phillipe, isn't it? Yes…, Phillipe, the vet from the Reserve."

"I can't believe it," I said, shocked.

"What's wrong, John?" Roger asked.

"That man down there is the same one who was carrying a briefcase full of money at Gajha the other night. That bastard is the informer who gives UMAG and the government all the right information. It's clear now that he's been behind all of this. We've got to advise Mummbar and Turner straight away."

"Ok, calm down, John," Roger told me. "As soon as we get to Dodoma, I'll ring my father. But just cool it now. There's nothing you can do up here. His moment will come. And if what you're saying is true, I'll take care of him myself."

The plane rose above the vast savanna, and as I stared at the extraordinary landscape below, the only thought I had in my head was disbelief. I simply couldn't believe that Phillipe was a traitor. I kept going over everything that had happened, the whole thing bothering me to such an extent that I wanted the plane to turn around and go back. I wanted to beat the truth out of Phillipe, but I knew that wasn't possible now.

Shinyanga was disappearing behind us and a few minutes later the enormous gold mine appeared threateningly on the horizon, reminding me of the two good men who had died there, for a cause that nobody could say would ever bear fruit. I rested my hand on the window that separated me from Gajha, grinding my teeth, hoping the battle would someday be over.

I looked back at the never-ending savanna, dotted with low trees, grass and scrub, stretching as far as the eye could see. It was here that the first human beings had lived, and thinking that, I was suddenly perplexed by the symbiosis that the first of our kind had had here with the vastness around me.

The thought of the immense sweep of time relaxed me, as I watched two lions mating below. My fury had ebbed, at least for now, and in the spectacle that the savanna is, we were flying now over a group of leopards, dashing away from the sound of our propeller. We were well above the plains but our presence frightened a herd of blue wildebeests that had been moving peacefully through the scrub. I could sense, from my seat in the sky, that there'd soon be a great feast below. And despite the fact that the leopards were running now in the opposite direction to the wildebeests, I knew it wouldn't be long before that changed. Our being here, had only delayed the inevitable for a couple of hours.

It was moments like these when nature's perfect order was easy to see. Only a few days before, Turner had talked about that. But it seemed to have special significance right now. The numbers staring at me across the savanna, the puzzle clearer. A hundred prey to one predator, the ecosystem balancing on that fine edge.

But thinking of the world of men beside that, it turned my stomach. Everything was unnatural, imbalanced. Man against man, man against every animal that lived. Man, ultimately, against himself.

The mad rush for lust and power, and everything in its path trampled underneath. It was a chilling thought, and showed how quickly my mind could shift from profound to base. I looked back through the window and imagined Marie's smile. I closed my eyes, leaning back in my seat, wondering what my life would be like without her, when I returned to England.

But suddenly, I was brought back to the present with a jolt as the plane hit a pocket of turbulence and was rocked from side to side, and jerked up and down, as we were almost dragged out of our seat belts.

Jamal was gripping the wheel like a vice as he inspected the instrument panel in front of him. Obviously nervous, he tapped the altimeter with the tip of his finger, as the indicator needle span in both directions. " What's going on, Jamal?" Roger asked, unnerved by the pilot's reaction.

"Something's wrong," he answered, staring at the front propeller. "We're losing height and I can't keep the plane stable."

I looked through the small window beside me and

noticed that part of the left wing had been torn and was fluttering like a leaf on the point of coming off the fuselage.

"The wing's coming apart," I screamed at Jamal.

"Shit, that's all I need. Why's everybody so irresponsible and stubborn."

"Who are you talking about?" Roger demanded to know.

"Your father, who else could it be? I told him this plane was only for short flights. But he wouldn't listen to me."

Roger nodded, an angry snarl forming on his face. "The old bastard will never learn."

Jamal tried to make radio contact and after several attempts, a hoarse voice came over the line. "We have to make a forced landing," he screamed into the transmitter. "One hundred and eighty-five kilometres north east of Shinyanga, heading for Dodoma."

Suddenly, the line went dead, as we lost altitude, the mighty savanna below looming up towards us. I unclenched my hand from the seat behind and worked on my panic, breathing deeply, and leaning forward with my eyes closed, crossing myself for the first and possibly the last time.

CHAPTER
TWENTY

After being unconscious for a time I couldn't determine, with a sharp pain rising through my forehead and a wild throbbing in my right leg, I started to emerge from a blurry consciousness.

The landing started to come back to me. The wing being ripped off, along with almost everything else on that side of the plane. We'd crashed through scrubland, and now as I sat up and looked around, I could see the cabin was incrusted with thorns. The pain interrupted me again, and looking down I saw the lower leg of my denim trousers, completely covered in blood. Everything was spinning around me. I put my hands back on my head, closed my eyes, thoughts of the others, making me reopen them straight away.

Jamal was immobile in his seat, his head hanging down, both arms dangling at his side. I heard a puff that distracted my attention to Roger, who was finding it hard to breathe.

After fighting for several minutes against my own pain, I unclipped the seat belt, and lifting myself up, discovered that my leg was ripped. I grimaced, and then let out a scream that echoed through my head. I closed my eyes again, trying to get some mental control over the pitiful state I was in, and a few seconds later, dragged myself to the seats ahead.

I put my hand on Jamal's neck and confirmed there was no pulse, and noticed that his eyes were still open. Startled, I lost balance and fell back again into my seat. And sitting there panting, I started to realize how bad the situation was.

I stayed where I was for a while, not wanting to move, grappling with the delirium of my pain, until I was brought back to reality by Roger's almost inaudible voice. "Are you all right, John?"

"No!" I told him flatly. "And you?"

"Bad!" he mumbled, his voice disappearing somewhere in his throat. "I don't see me getting out of this."

In spite of the pain that was drilling through my leg, I leaned forward again, and saw that a piece of metal was sticking out of his left lung. As soon as I saw it there, I realized he was dying. I looked at it closely, not knowing what to do. If I tried to pull it out, he would surely bleed to death in a matter of seconds. And if the blood loss didn't kill him, the pain would.

Jamal was dead and Roger was dying. The only thing I could think of doing, was to look through the window at the endless savanna around me. I thought *radio*, in the blur of my thoughts, but discovered straight away that it had been smashed to bits in the landing. "John, you've got to stay strong," Roger's pained voice advised me. "Don't give up. Keep fighting until they find you."

I knew that I was listening to a man's last words. He could barely speak, but he had to get something off his chest. "I ask you, if you're lucky enough to get out of this, to tell my father that I'm sorry we didn't say goodbye to each other in Gambala. I wanted to hurt him... like he'd hurt me in the past."

His voice seemed to be getting weaker with every word, but in spite of everything, my pain, his agony, I was held in the grip of his desperate effort to be heard.

"I never forgave him for leaving my mother and me, when he first came to Africa. I was only ten years old, and my father thought that by sending us money everything would be all right. He devoted himself to saving wildlife in the north of Tanzania, and had become a hero. Saving animals was the most important thing in his life..." He stopped talking, coughed, opened his mouth to speak again, but coughed instead. I didn't know what to do. I felt like telling him to stop trying to talk. But life was ebbing out of him, and words were all he had.

"After having lived all my life in Edinburgh, I studied law in Germany, my mother's country. Then I came to Africa to work near my father. Ironic, isn't it?"

"I don't know what to say, Roger. The truth is..."

"I'm running out of time, John!" he grunted like a wounded animal before it dies. "Save Peter, look for the papers in my case, and tell my father that despite everything, I know he loved me in his own way. Tell him not to blame himself for what's happened here."

I watched the tears running down his face, saw him close his eyes. "Take him in your arms and tell him... what I said here."

And then he was gone.

I put my hands on my head. Fear had unchained

objectivity. I couldn't face the truth of my own life, but now, in these horrible last minutes of Roger's life, everything had become clearer. He would never know it, but Roger had taught me in a few minutes, the true meaning of life.

I sat there staring at the two dead bodies in front of me. I'd never felt so alone. I was at the mercy of an inhospitable land, infested with insects and wild animals. I could only hope that someone had marked the spot on the map that Jamal had transmitted in those last desperate seconds.

Time had creaked to a halt. The silence in that cabin of death was overwhelming. And as each minute passed, I realized that no nightmare could equal this reality. I needed to find a way out.

I looked around, trying to decide what my next move should be, lifting my trouser leg up, and studying the deep cut, I found a sharp bone splinter sticking out from my shinbone. Blood flowed steadily out, covering all the lower part of my leg. I breathed deeply, tried to calm down, to let clear thought prevail. I stretched the seat belt that was hanging at my side, and holding it in my hands, I ripped it from its support and tied it tightly around my leg, to stem the flow of blood.

I looked around the cabin for a first-aid kit or something else that could kill the pain, and stop the risk of infection. But there was nothing. I dragged myself across the cabin and out through the hole on the other side. The temperature had been climbing steadily and I needed to find some shade. I didn't have the least idea of what fate had in store for me, I only knew with my leg the way it was, that I couldn't go too far.

And standing there, propping myself up on the

wreck of the Cessna, surrounded by an angry savanna, I felt somehow that I would survive. I tried to walk, but the pain doubled me up and I fell hard onto the ground, lying there prostrate, dust in my mouth and the sun's rays beating into my back.

I don't know how long I lay there, gasping like a wounded animal, but my head shot up suddenly when I heard a loud snort. I looked around, my vision still blurred, trying to make out what had made the sound, and saw through the bushes, a dark undefined shape coming straight towards me.

CHAPTER
TWENTY-ONE

I squinted, trying to discern what it was that was coming towards me, and in a flash I forgot the pain in my leg, as my eyes confirmed a black rhinoceros about to charge.

I dragged myself up, and looked back over my shoulder at the plane, that was completely open on the side I was on. I edged backwards, until I was a few yards from the Cessna, then span around and ran as fast as I could, rounding the front propeller to the other side, where the wing was reclined diagonally on the ground. And with nowhere else to go, I wedged myself into the small space between the fuselage and the wing.

The rhinoceros began to batter the other side of my hiding place, the plane rattling like a toy. I pressed my face against the propeller. I felt that this interminable war was going to finish me off sooner or later.

After what seemed like a long time of hiding there with my heart in my throat, the sudden silence distracted me. I strained my ears, but could hear nothing, and just hoped that the rhinoceros had tired of not finding an aggressor to fight.

I lay on the ground, exhausted. It was midday and the temperature was still rising, and from what little I could see around the plane, there was no sign of water.

I closed my eyes, and let my mind run over the contents of the cabin, trying to locate a canteen, or any liquid that could quench my thirst. Almost an hour had passed since the enraged rhino had stopped butting the plane, and finally I dragged myself out, looking around everywhere for any sign of the beast.

But there was nothing to see; he'd left. I steadied myself on the aircraft, and without taking my hand off, hobbled in extreme pain, around to the cabin, and sat down inside, behind the two dead bodies, that now after the battering that the plane had taken, were flung over their seats. I leaned back, trying to relax as I went over the tortuous thoughts that unconsciously were going round and round in my mind. The only thing I had certain at that moment was that I had to stay alive until the imaginary search party arrived and before my leg became infected.

I looked around the cabin again for something to drink and saw beside the pilot's seat a plastic bottle with a thick, orange liquid inside. I dragged myself over and undoing the top, smelt its contents desperately. The sweet aroma told me it was some sort of tropical fruit drink, which I sipped straight away, experiencing the inexplicable pleasure of papaya juice in my mouth.

I closed my eyes and took little sips, trying to prolong the pleasure in my palate, but seconds later, I realized sadly that the bottle was empty. I looked at it. Held it up in the air, tried to drain a few more precious drops out, but I was only sucking air. I threw it on the floor, cursing. I looked in every nook and cranny of the cabin for something else to drink, but there was nothing. It seemed I'd just drunk my last drop, and the grim thought of a long painful death began to do the rounds of my head.

The hours ticked by, it started to get dark and I knew that night was not far off. I looked for a lantern but only found a cigarette lighter beside the pilot's seat.

The heat inside the cabin was unbearable, so I went back to my hiding place under the wing, lay down on my back, closed my eyes, and in a blur of terrible thoughts, and exhausted, I fell asleep.

I had no way of knowing how long I'd been asleep, but when I woke up, I was shivering, my forehead was covered in sweat and dripping down my face onto my shirt. It was minutes to sunset, the light grey, the air muggy, as I peered out.

I was only a few minutes away from whatever the night would bring: nocturnal predators, scavengers. I quivered, took a deep breath wondering what to do, when the thought of scavengers made me think of the two dead bodies sitting there in the cabin. How long would it take before their decomposing bodies attracted vultures or a pack of hyenas? Sooner or later something was bound to come for them. And the thought sent new shivers up my spine.

Roger deserved a decent Christian burial, and as devastating as it was going to be for his father to discover that his son had died here, it would be even worse to find out his dead body had been ripped to pieces by hyenas or his bones picked over by vultures.

I looked at my watch. It was nearly eight. I decided to open the exterior compartment that had become stuck by the impact of the crash. And after a few minutes of battling with the lever, I managed to open it. I took out my bag, put it on the ground, took some clothes out, and put it under the wing where I planned to spend the night.

Only a few minutes remained of dusk so I looked

at my leg again. The skin that circled the wound had turned purple and I reasoned that the tourniquet was too tight and cutting the circulation. It would more than likely turn gangrenous like that. But, if I released the pressure, I would probably bleed to death in a few hours. I decided to undo the knot to check the flow of blood and realized almost straight away that a great clot had formed around the wound which had reduced the hemorrhaging considerably. I tore one of the sleeves off the shirts I'd taken out of the bag and wound it around the tip of the bone that jutted out of my leg, and amid intense pain that ran right up my calf to my knee, I started to think about the possibility that if help didn't come soon, I would lose the leg. The thought paralyzed me and I lay still on the ground, desperately thirsty, the sensation that my mouth was full of sand.

I knew for the time being that there was nothing I could do. Night had fallen and if I was ever going to drink again, it would have to be in the morning.

I lay there for hours in the same position, imagining shapes coming out of the dark, going over the disaster of the accident, and the loss of another two lives. And my relentless questioning of the existence of God surprised me by storming back, making me think my lack of faith over. And for the first time in my life, I felt a knot in my throat, as the tears welling up in my eyes found nowhere to go. I felt indescribably unhappy, coming to terms with the fact that my world would be that much better if I was a believer. But my skepticism and inner rebellion had gagged me, and stopped any connection whatsoever with that spiritual world I needed so much.

I continued my journey through the past and in the blink of an eye, I was very small again, lost in the nostalgia of my childhood. I could see Gwyn clearly, sharing the good and bad moments so many years before.

I remembered the times when my father had come home drunk, and how we had fled that angry inebriated voice, running to the wardrobe in my bedroom, thinking that we would never be found there. And when he didn't drag us out of our hiding place, we would fall asleep on top of the shoes until our mother, after having survived one more battle, would carry us to our beds, and bless each of us, which for her was our protection against my father's bad moods.

In spite of being the son of such an exceptionally religious woman like my mother, I was never a believer. I reasoned that if God did in fact exist, then pain and evil would have no place in his world. But on seeing the perfection and magnificence of the world that lay in front of me, it was unquestionable that he, who had created such perfection, had to be a kind being, full of love and more powerful than human kind could conceive. Perhaps, he himself had granted my grandmother the grace of being able to receive and give love at the same time. I remembered her love of life, and knew that I missed her more than ever at that moment, and heard the words that she had repeated over and over to me, "The one who forgives, loves, and the one who loves, will be blessed by the light of God."

I was thankful for all the warmth and faith that had been placed in my heart like a seed in the earth, and which I felt was now beginning to germinate in me. And after a long fight between my conscience and that inner force that seemed to be clamouring for help, I lost consciousness for several hours.

I woke up with the strange sensation of goose bumps running up my leg, as high as my thigh, and holding my breath, and slowly taking the cigarette lighter out my pocket, I lit it over my chest, and froze with fear.

CHAPTER
TWENTY-TWO

I held my breath, tensed my arms, lifted the lighter, and shining it over my lower body, saw a giant brown scorpion with it claws raised. Attracted by the glow of the lighter that was reflected on its brilliant shell, it ran quickly up my chest, where I met it with the back of my hand, sending it flying through the air.

Shocked, I was forced out of my cramped space, dragging myself from under the wing, and standing up, I wandered around in circles like a zombie.

It was only a few hours to daybreak and the early morning cold had penetrated the thin pullover under my jacket, and chilled every bone in my body, making me shiver constantly.

In spite of feeling dizzy and weak, I walked away from the plane, pushed on by the absurd belief that I could find a safer place to spend the rest of the night. But after a dozen yards, my leg seized up, and I fell on the ground, the terrible rush of pain in the leg forcing a scream out of the depths of my soul, echoing through the immense black savanna around me.

I cursed having come to Africa again, to finish up like this, defeated almost, spitting sand, bleeding, as the mysterious and hostile veil of night choked what resistance was left out of me.

Nevertheless, there was something burning inside me that refused to give in. An instinct to live through this hell, a mind that was working its way through everything stacked against it. I figured I had a few days to do something before I would die of thirst or hunger, or before the infection finished me off.

There were so many things to do if I got out of this. I had to save Peter, to tell Turner what his son had said, to reveal the truth about Phillipe. I couldn't die here and now. There was still too much to do: to hold Marie in my arms once more, to see her smile, to live with her, to build a life together, to share for the first time in my life.

It was as if all my life was being replayed in slow motion, as I lay there. I could see all the mistakes I'd made, the people I'd left behind, the emptiness of my existence. My fears had made me an arrogant man, who lived only to satisfy his own selfishness, pushing me from one mistake to the next. Searching desperately and mistakenly for something that I vaguely imagined was waiting to be found inside me.

I had lived my life, a prisoner of my own loneliness, and here now, I lay wounded, lost and more alone than ever. It was almost as if I could hear Mike out there somewhere saying: "This is your karma." My last breaths would come soon, and in my terrible loneliness, a tiny being prostrated in the great vastness around it, I would die, just as I had lived.

I felt dispirited and depressed, and with my stomach shrunken, remembered with embarrassment how arrogant I had been a few hours before in thinking that I wouldn't die here. For some time, now I had been putting my feet into that hell that I'd first heard of when I was a child; that purgatory after death, where we would pay for our sins in pain and eternal suffering. The fire from that abysmal cauldron was consuming me slowly, and now I felt as defenceless and frightened as a child, in the middle of a strange new world.

I had travelled bravely, along a long road of my own choosing, but now had dropped my guard and felt completely vulnerable. I understood that I could no longer dwell on my own past. I opened my heart, and in complete humility, began to direct my words to the Almighty, lamenting the fact that I had been incapable of sensing his magnificence, and had suffered as a result. I asked him to free me from my remorse and all the grudges that I had carried for so long, and especially the contained rage that I felt all that time. I begged him to forgive me for the pain that I'd caused to so many people as well as to myself. And immersed in my confession and in my own regret in this unusual conversation with God, I began to feel much calmer. I hoped that feeling would last until I died.

My fears were leaving me slowly. It was incredible, but despite the panorama of what lay ahead of me and the pain in my leg, that had me at times on the edge of madness, I decided to trust in what fate had in store for me.

I lay on the ground, and stared up at the immensity of the starry sky that seemed to be beckoning me. And after hours of silent reflection, finally the first rays of light appeared on the horizon.

I tried to sit up, feeling dizzy and nauseous. I looked at my leg again, noting that there was a reddish ring around the wound. It looked as if the infection had increased and, worried, I recovered it with the scrap of material and hobbled back to the plane, hoping naively that I would soon be rescued.

I was desperately thirsty and could feel that my stomach had contracted from hunger. I looked around the aircraft and saw a group of meerkats, standing on two feet, watching every one of my movements. Suddenly aware that I had seen them, they dashed off to hide in their burrows, a couple of small heads sticking out of the ground.

I continued my laboured progress back to the plane, but froze before I reached it, when I only saw Roger's body in the cabin. Jamal had gone without leaving a trace. I looked around, in a panic, and in the distance under a tree, saw what was left of Jamal underneath three vultures. There was no point in expending any more energy in going over to do battle with the big, black birds. So I limped my way into the cabin and covered my face in disgust. It seemed things were taking a turn for the worse.

I looked at my watch; it was nearly nine in the morning. Time was passing with incredible slowness and the silence across the savanna seemed to be my worst enemy. I closed my eyes, trying to disconnect myself from this crude reality, and thought about that night in Marie's room when we'd made love, and fell asleep with the memory of her in my arms.

CHAPTER
TWENTY-THREE

After I woke up from replacing my grim reality with the thought of Marie's warm body under the sheets, the first thing I saw was Roger's head drooped beside me. I took my jacket off and put it over his head, and started wondering how I could save his body from the same fate as Jamal's.

I got out of the plane again and started browsing around the crash site for something useful. It didn't take me long to find a part of the wing wedged in the branches of a spiny bush. The size looked perfect for what I had in mind but I couldn't budge it with my hands, so I walked over to another tree and broke a long branch off, with the idea of using it to pry the wing off the bush. But as I dragged myself towards the metal sheet, using the branch as a walking stick, the heat seemed to get the better of me, and it felt as if the sun's rays were piercing my head, as I began to stagger across the ground, my mind spinning. I had to stop and take a few deep breaths;

I could feel my heart beating irregularly, a film of cold sweat forming on my neck as if the sweat was there to put the fire in my head out.

In the middle of my torment, my eyes suddenly opened wider as I saw two lionesses and three of their cubs passing across the horizon, apparently unaware of my presence. Worn out, I made it to the bush, and putting the branch into the thick tangle of thorns, I pushed the wing until it fell free the other side. I went round as quickly as I could and started dragging the heavy wing back to the plane. It would have been difficult to move even if I was in good condition, but under the circumstances, I don't know how I managed to get it back there, and when I finally did, collapsed on the fuselage, trying to find the strength to get into the cabin and lift the wing in after me.

But suddenly, a roar behind my back paralyzed me, and with a surge of adrenalin streaming through my body, I span around to see several lionesses moving towards me about fifty yards away. With extraordinary agility, I slipped into the cabin and somehow managed to lift the wing in after me, fitting it like a master craftsman into the hollowed out cabin, as I heard another roar on the other side of the wing, and through a small space that the metal hadn't covered, saw a threatening eye looking into mine.

In the next few seconds, I fought with all the strength I had left, to keep the wing in place, as the lioness fought to pry it off, and the small plane rocked with the effort, until pulling the sheet of metal a little further towards me then pushing back with all my force, I rammed the lioness on the head, and roaring her discontent, she left me and the plane alone.

In the silence that followed, it felt like my heart would pound its way out of my chest. This land that had seemed like paradise only a few days before, now was nothing more than a battle field where only the fittest survived. I had found strength that I didn't know that I had, but that was now spent after the effort of fighting the lion off.

I lay back inside the cabin, my shoulders slumped, my eyes closed, going over the list of things that were likely to kill me in the next couple of days. At least for now, the broken wing would protect me where I was, but there was nothing to drink and thirst was the most likely candidate to finish me off. My body was already dehydrating and I had to find something to drink, even if it were only a few drops, before it was too late.

I looked around the cabin again, and saw a plastic bag rolled up under Roger's seat. I reached out and pulled it towards me, the memory of a television program, appearing suddenly in my mind. And holding the plastic bag in my hand, I brought the scene of desert survival back from the depths of the past. I could see a pair of hands digging a hole in the sand, a container inserted inside and covered with plastic on the surface, held down by rocks on its four edges, a stone in the center of the plastic sheet above.

I nodded, going over the scene again, remembering in amazement that the heat of the day would condense whatever humidity there was into vapour that would drip down into the container.

With an almost destroyed pole that was sticking out of the cabin, I dislodged the metal base in which Jamal carried his bottle of water and got out of the plane, looking around for any sign of the lioness. She was gone, but two warthogs were watching me as they crossed the brush not far away, but after a few seconds they lost interest in me and went on their way. I continued on with the task I'd set myself, breaking four branches off a tree and sitting down on the ground, digging a hole, covering it with plastic and leaving the stone on the top, I hoped that there would be some humidity to make the whole thing work.

After I'd followed all the steps and was satisfied that everything was in order, I went back to the plane, got in, pulled the wing back into place behind me, and lay down on the two rear seats to shelter from the burning sun. My breathing was heavy and blocked. The heat was bothering me to such an extent that I could feel it climbing up my legs and come to rest like a ball of fire in my head, which I now imagined to be a helium balloon that would explode at any moment.

My head was dripping sweat, and in that metal oven a few hours later, I found that I was floating in my own bodily fluids. I knew my survival time had been abruptly reduced. I could hardly move, burning up with fever, the relentless malaise running through my body, as if I'd been poisoned.

Shivering and trembling, I forced myself to sit up, leaning forward and supporting my weight on the makeshift door. And after calming myself a little, I put all my weight on the wing, and pushing, knocked it onto the ground. I had no idea what the temperature was outside, perhaps 40 °C, but the hot breeze felt like a blast of frozen air over my body. But rather than stand there, and enjoy the sudden change in temperature, I walked quickly and desperately to the moisture collector, hoping in a blur of hysteria, that I would find traces of water.

I lifted the stone up and looking below the plastic layer, saw in a sudden burst of euphoria that some drops of water lay at the bottom of the container. I took it out and careful not to spill any of its precious contents, lifted it to my mouth and took the only sip there was. It felt as if my cracked lips had hardly been wet, and I looked angrily back into the empty container, lifting it up and shaking it over my desperate mouth.

The weather continued the same way without any sign in the sky above of a search plane. I'd almost given up hope now, and wasn't too far short of being resigned to my fate. This new depression made it even harder to cope with the weakened state I was in, and I zigzagged my way across the burning ground, without knowing where I was going, walking like a living dead man until I sat down in the shade of a thorny tree.

I looked down at a large rock beside me and turned it over, to find a seething mass of earth worms and white larva writhing underneath. Repulsed at the sight and still nauseous, I forced myself to pick the fattest and most nutritious worm out, and dangling it in the air above me, closed my eyes and put it in my mouth. I could feel it twisting as I crunched into the peculiar texture of its skin, biting though its life, and then chewing its disagreeable earthy taste. I felt like vomiting, but knew that this grub could give me a little more energy to face this hellish battle to survive. I looked back down at the rest of them, scurrying every which way as if they knew that one of them would be the next to go.

After a true vomitive feast and careful not to be pricked by any of the dozens of thorns in the tree I lay down and fell asleep, I woke up again when the sun had almost set, leaving a thick orange smear with traces of lilac across the sky. But the beauty of that moment was lost on me, as I reflected on the end of the day and a long night plagued with predators, ahead of me. All of them in search of prey.

I dragged myself back to the plane, entered and sealed it behind me, smelling the strong stench of Roger's rotting body. Feeling nauseous again, and without knowing what else to do, I closed my eyes. My exhausted body seemed to have entered a turbine, throbbing from the point of my toes to the last neuron of my brain. I started to become delirious, which provoked a painful contraction in my stomach that made me vomit compulsively, plunging my mind into a turbid, nauseous world.

Hours, or even days passed, where I seemed to be only conscious for minutes. I remembered, between dreams, that a rusty panel covered the roof of the cabin and a tangle of cables hung down above me. Submerged and lost in a deep stupor, I was brought back to reality by a blinding flash of light, as I vaguely made two figures out, standing above me with the light behind them. "John, John…"

Without being able to see the features of their faces, I stammered, "We're dead!"

"No, John," I heard a deep, grave voice say, and felt the touch of a hand on my arm. " You're alive, Lad."

The only thing I remembered then was that someone dragged me heavily by the feet and I lay on a flat surface while the rays of the sun dazzled me, forcing me to keep my eyes tightly shut.

"Can you hear me, John? Everything's going to be all right." A voice insisted, as I felt an object on my lips and liquid in my mouth. But being unable to swallow, I felt it spilling over my neck, making me feel as if I was drowning. Then everything went dark and I saw myself going quietly, towards a light that illuminated a long corridor.

CHAPTER
TWENTY-FOUR

When I regained consciousness, I found myself lying in a dimly-lit room where the window was partly covered by a broken Persian blind. I could see all sorts of catheters and cables connecting my body to a loud monitor that produced an irritating, irregular sound.

Even though my eyelids were heavy, I was able to run my eye around the room stopping on someone sitting in a corner with their head bent down. When I tried to speak, I realized that a green plastic tube that connected me to a respirator was sticking out of my mouth. I waved my hand and grunted, and succeeded to attract the attention of whoever it was seated there.

"John!" a surprised voice said.

Trying to respond, my voice seemed locked in my chest. After a few minutes, an entourage of people dressed in white coats filed into the room, as one of the strange group listened to my heart and lungs with a stethoscope, then, suddenly, someone else took my jaw and extracted an inner tube from my throat. I didn't know where I was, or who these people were, and asked with a strong burning rasp in my vocal chords. "Where am I?"

"You're in Shinyanga hospital," one of them informed me, slowly elevating the head of the bed. "How do you feel, John?"

"I don't know," I answered confused and weak, as my heart missed a beat when I saw Marie step forward from the group of black faces.

"Oh, John!" she said putting both hands over her mouth. "I can't believe you're back after such a long time."

"Such a long time?" I enquired, still confused.

The doctors stepped back and said they would wait outside as Marie sat on the bed at my side, took my hand and began to explain what happened. "When we rescued you, almost four days after the accident, you fell into a coma. And…" She paused. "You've been asleep for a little more than three months."

"What?" I said, shocked. "It can't be true? And Roger? Did you recover the body?"

Marie nodded. "Yes, but it was horrible to find him like that. We were able to bury him in Gambala. His father has been completely devastated by what's happened."

"I can imagine," I said, taking her hand. "It was without any doubt the worst experience of my life. I never thought you'd find us. And Peter? Was he rescued?"

Marie looked down, bit her lower lip, and said nothing.

"What happened, Marie? Tell me, please. Was he rescued?"

"I'm sorry, John," she said, rubbing the back of her hand, looking away. "Peter died."

I didn't know what I felt at that moment. Shock was not exactly the word. I'd woken up from a sleep that had lasted three months, to find out my old mate, Peter, was dead. I was overwhelmed. I needed Marie to tell me it wasn't true. "Are you sure he's dead? Who told you? Who recovered the body?"

"Turner received a call around two months ago from the State Prison, where they confirmed he'd…"

"He'd been what?" I said in disbelief.

"That he'd been killed in a fight by one of the other prisoners. It was a terrible shock to us all then. Just as it is now, telling you what happened again."

I watched her get up off the bed. I had no idea where she was going. And it appeared that neither did she, as she started lapping the bed.

"And his body, was that recovered?"

I guessed she knew that question was coming as she stopped at the foot of the bed. "We found out too late, John. His body had already been taken to a common grave."

"What? What are you telling me? Where were Mike and Turner all that time?"

"You can't blame them, John. They never stopped looking for him. They went everywhere trying to find him," she said shaking her head. "No, you can't blame them. As far as I can make out, the bastards behind all of that moved Peter around from one place to the next. To tell you the truth, we all thought Peter had been killed before he actually was."

I was crying by the time she'd finished telling me what had happened to him. I wanted something, justice perhaps, but I could barely lift my arms. All I could do was cry. "And Pete's wife? Was she told?"

"Mike went back to England a few months ago to tell her personally. And since then, he's rung almost every day to see how you're doing. It's been pitiful to see Mike the way he is. He hasn't got over what happened to Peter and he's been worried sick about you!"

I hardly had the strength to speak; a new wave of emptiness was sweeping over me. "I have to get out of here, Marie. Not just this bed, but out of Africa. I have to get back to London as soon as possible." And while trying to get into a more comfortable position, I was suddenly paralyzed with fear.

CHAPTER
TWENTY-FIVE

Marie came towards me with her face contorted as I ran my hands over my leg. "My leg! My leg!" I stammered, as what happened on the savanna came storming back. "My God. Why?"

For the first time in my life, I cried uncontrollably. "When did that happen?"

Marie looked lost for words, but finally said, "I understand what you must be going through."

"There's no way you can understand," I said, desperately trying to come to grips with this shock, an hour after I'd come to. I was starting to think it would have been better to have stayed in a coma. Or death was another option. "No one can understand."

"I know what you're saying is true. But I want to try and share the pain with you. It was a miracle that you didn't lose all the leg. You can't imagine the state we found you in that day. We knew how terrible it would be for you, but they had to…"

"Amputate my leg!" I said, spitting the words out, as I ran my hand over the stump of my knee. "How could you have let them do that, Marie? It would have been better to let me die."

"I know what I'm saying is hard to take," she said wiping the tears off her cheeks with the back of her hand. "But you are more than your leg, John. Your spirit, your heart, your mind is what makes you who you are. And you're alive. That wouldn't have been possible any other way."

"I don't want anyone to feel sorry for me. Especially you, Marie. I think it's better that you go now. I don't want you to look at me this way," I said, staring at the window. "Just leave me alone!"

"Very well, John," she said, picking her bag up and walking straight to the door. "I'll leave you alone today, because I know you need time to take in everything you've just heard. But I'll be back tomorrow, and I warn you, I won't let you tell me to go away, ever again."

After she left, I fell into a black mood that seemed to last hours, and beaten, I was sucked into a series of light and meaningless dreams, until I woke up again around midnight, dizzy, feeling sick and covered in sweat. I looked for a bell in the darkness to ring the night nurse and she came with a plastic tray. I vomited twice and after wiping my face, she put a thermometer in my mouth. "You're okay," she said a few minutes later, before she left the room. "There's no fever."

I felt more alone than I had on the savanna after the nurse left the room, forcing me, once again, to confront my inner ghosts. The new me was a one-legged man who'd lost three months of his life in a coma, and who in the dark of his lonely single bed, was ravaged by visions of his best friend being beaten to death in jail. It was heavy stuff to come to terms with, the first day back.

As the days went by, I became resigned to my fate. I knew I couldn't change anything and besides the overwhelming clarity of that observation, I also thought a lot about what had happened to me on the savanna. I knew something had changed in me out there alone, staring my own oblivion in the face.

During the rehabilitation process in the hospital, Marie visited me constantly along with Mummbar and Turner, who'd fallen into a deep depression that he didn't look like coming out of any time soon. On one of the many occasions when Turner and I were alone, I told him what Roger had asked me to tell him. I reached out to him and told him this was the hug Roger had wanted to give him, and the two of us embraced on the bed and he cried in my arms. It was an extraordinarily moving moment, which made me feel that my problems were small set against his.

"I'm sorry, Roger," he said, as if his son were in the room with us, and slowly pulling himself away from me, he wiped his tears on his shirt sleeve, and walked to the window and stared out in silence. "Thanks, John. I appreciated that. It was very important for me to hear that Roger had forgiven me before he died."

He continued to stare out the window and I imagined that, what had just happened between us had helped to bring him back a little from the lonely cell of his thoughts. Maybe he'd even seen the flicker of a light at the end of the tunnel. I left him like that for a few minutes before I said, "I know this isn't the moment to give you anything else to worry about, but…"

"Tell me," he said, turning around.

"There's something you need to know about Phillipe."

"What are you talking about?"

"Did you know that Phillipe was the man who was with Dormonth that night on the Gajha airfield? The same one carrying the briefcase with the money, remember him?"

Turner was shaking his head. "How do you know it was him?"

"The red jacket with the yellow trim. A man was standing on the Shinyanga airfield the day we took off, wearing the same jacket. Jamal recognized him. Remember that everyone's got their price. It would seem Phillipe's found his."

"I can't believe it, John. You must have confused him with someone else. He's a respectable doctor, a professional. He's been with me for years."

"Appearances can be deceptive. I'm sure there's more to him than meets the eye. But it's up to you to find out the truth. Just remember what I've told you."

My words had knocked Turner for six. He was breathing heavily and frowning.

"Phillippe went back to Belgium a month ago to visit his family. He won't be back for another couple of months. I'll look into what you've just told me, and if it's true, I'll fix it my way," he paused. "The only thing I ask you is, not to tell any of this to Marie or anyone else, until we know it's true."

"No problem. I'll leave it up to you."

CHAPTER
TWENTY-SIX

I left Shinyanga Hospital a week and a half later, supported on a pair of wooden crutches that I'd already learnt to use skillfully, and went back to rest on the Reserve. And rest was what I needed! There were so many things to come to terms with now that I only had one leg, not the least of which was facing the fact that I'd be like this for the rest of my life. Not only was walking difficult, but I found it hard to look at myself in the mirror. I spent most of my time looking inwards, searching for an angle that would help me cope with the way I was now. And slowly, with Marie's help, I started to work my way back towards the semblance of the old me.

In the hospital, Peter's death had been a terrible load to bear, but it really sank in back at Gambala. No jokes, none of those great moments together, drinking beer and telling old stories. That was all gone, and the thought of how he'd died was with me most of the time, along with a festering desire for revenge.

My relationship with Marie was getting stronger all the time, and a new bond had formed between us. I knew it wasn't just because I felt crippled nor for the immense gratitude that I had for her. It was way more than that.

The purpose of my stay at Gambala, was to build my strength up for my return to London, however, it was good to be back on the Reserve, being near the animals and getting to see Nina again. She had grown enormously, but despite not having seen me for more than three months, she recognized me immediately. When I touched her, she cried desperately, making me smile for the first time since I'd left. I picked her up, like a real father would his daughter, after returning from a long trip abroad, and held her in the air for a few seconds, as she stretched her arms out pleadingly towards me. I pulled her to my chest and after rubbing her head in my pullover, with extraordinary curiosity, she began to delouse the interior of my growing beard with her wrinkled fingers.

Once she'd got a tray and some utensils for shaving, Marie began to cut my unruly hair, the locks beginning to fall everywhere on the floor. "Christ, I don't think I've ever been as hairy as this in my whole life. My hair had grown that long that I was beginning to look like one of the many lions I'd seen on the savanna."

Marie smiled on hearing my attempt at humor, which had been picking up speed in the last week or so. As she swept the hair into a tidy pile in the corner, I watched her vaporous white dress, her curves, her breasts protruding from below her neckline. When she came back to the seat I was sitting on, I freed one of my hands from holding Nina on my lap and ran it around Marie's waist, pulling her to me—about to kiss her stomach—but she pulled away, holding the scissors in the air. "What are your intentions, Jonathan Carmichael?"

"Perverse!" I answered, with my eyes half-closed, smiling, and pulling her back to me, kissing her, feeling her moist lips on my mine, her warm breath. "I'll be back soon for you, Darling. The thought of even being away from you for a day is killing me. "I paused, held in a twilight zone of sentiment and passion. "I love you."

Marie sat down on the bed beside me and leaning towards me, said, "I love you, too, John, but our lives are so different, in every sense of the word." She sighed, holding my hand tightly. "I think it will be difficult to combine our different ways of life. Like I told you a long time ago, I've chosen this life, and decided to stay here. This is and will continue to be the main thing in my life, Johnny. I belong here. This is my home."

Disheartened by her words and thinking again about moving from London to Gambala, I felt suddenly edgy and trapped by circumstances that seemed bigger than our feelings. I began to wonder how I'd cope on my own back in England without her support and love. I couldn't measure what she'd done for me here on the Reserve, and felt the sudden chill that our separation was going to bring. She was the only woman I'd felt capable of giving everything up for. "Mike and I will be finished there soon. We will have dismantled UMAG and get justice for what happened to Peter. But I swear to you, that I'll be back."

"It's good that we talked about this, John," she said, walking over to a chest of drawers, taking my camera out of one. "I asked Mike to leave this with me, because I knew that you'd wake up one morning and wonder where it was."

"Thanks, Marie," I said, taking a few shots of her, thinking that when I was a child, I'd thought the image and its essence would stay with me forever. "When I come back, as far as I can see, I'll have to look after all the monkeys on the Reserve, because I've become an expert in changing nappies and giving them milk bottles."

"We'll see when you come back," she sighed, going over what we'd just said, picking up the scissors again. "One thing I do know is that you'd make a good father."

After she'd finished cutting my hair and beard, we left Nina in the youngsters' common cage, and watched her become the leader in a matter of minutes. I couldn't stop smiling to see her giving orders to the rest, remembering that day I'd found her dying near the lake. Her life had turned a full circle.

"She looks like her mother," I said, laughing.

Marie, raising her eyebrows, and staring at me, flashed me a smile.

After two weeks resting and feeling better physically and spiritually, thanks to Marie, who didn't leave my side for a minute, the day finally arrived to return home to England. Fortunately, I didn't have the equipment to worry about, as Mike had already taken it with him. I was going to travel light, with a small bag and a camera swung over my neck.

The night before my return, I spoke with Turner again about Phillipe, advising him that on my return to London I would investigate him completely, because I didn't want to make any more accusations without having tangible proof behind me. These were serious allegations, involving corruption, aiding and abetting murders and torture. I needed something more substantial before proceeding any further.

Mike had already set things in motion, with regard to the general environmental damage, alerting the press and advising the United Nations Organization. But my arrival in London was going to have a bigger impact on everyone, Gwyn and Mike included.

Turner was exhausted physically and emotionally. Nothing mattered to him now after the death of his son. He was that far gone in his depression that it appeared that nothing could bring him back. His face seemed to be permanently set in stone and his conversation was kept tight and to the point, without any humor or sense of wanting to get on with the job. Mummbar on the other hand, was even more determined than before, if that was possible, and seemed to have taken Turner's workload on his shoulders as well as his own.

"John, we all regret what's happened," Turner said to me that last night before I left. Not only have you lost a leg, but also your best friend. We'll always be in your debt here at Gambala."

I thanked him and shook his hand. His expression told me he still felt guilty and no amount of talking was going to fix that. It seemed like an unbearable load to carry. "All this has had its effect on you, too, Bill. You can't go on like this. You've got to turn the corner just like I've had to. There's a lot to do here, and many lives depend on your will to see all this mess cleaned up. I want to thank you for what you've done for me in these last few months and I'd feel a lot better if I knew you weren't going to give up. We can't change what's happened. But we can change what's happening here."

He nodded, a trace of a smile parting his lips, hugging me lightly, as Mummbar came in to tell me he'd take me to the airport in Dar es Salaam personally.

"You should take all this with you," Mummbar said, lifting a pile of papers up from his desk. "All the papers that were in the Cessna that day are here, including Peter's passport. I'm sure his wife would want to keep it."

I took it from him and put it in my back pocket. "Thanks, I'm sure you're right."

I said my farewells to everybody on the Reserve, especially Nina, because I was afraid that when I came back a few months later she wouldn't recognize me. I could never have imagined six months before, how important an animal could become to me. She just looked at me curiously without having any idea what I was thinking.

I stayed with Marie to the very last minute the next morning, leaving my music tape with her, telling her that when she listened to each of the songs I'd be with her in spirit, and I promised her once again that I would return soon. I gave her a long kiss, and let her perfume seep into my memory. That scent would stay with me for months or until I saw her again. I felt thankful that I'd found the woman of my life. And without being able to say or express my feelings any more deeply, I got into the jeep with Mummbar, put my crutches on the floor, and closed the door behind me.

Marie was standing at the window with Nina in her arms. "I'm going to miss you terribly, John."

"The same goes for me. You know that. Look after yourself and Nina, too. Remember I'm only a call away," I called out, pretending to hold a receiver to my ear as Bantu drove off, leaving the two of them lost in a trail of dust.

CHAPTER
TWENTY-SEVEN

There was another pilot waiting for us at Shinyanga airfield when we arrived. He seemed pleased to see me. "Mister John, it's good to see you're better. You don't know me but I was the pilot the day you were found."

"Thanks for telling me," I said cutting him off, before he started talking too much about what had happened to me out there on the savanna.

He apparently sensed my discomfort, and looked away from my crutches. "I'm sorry, Mister John. Don't worry about anything this time. This plane's in perfect condition."

I sighed. "I hope so, my friend."

Mummbar took the pilot aside, and after going over the details of the flight with him, came back to the plane. "Everything's in order, John. Don't give this flight a second thought."

I'd already done more than that and had an uneasy

déjà-vu feeling about the whole thing. And not only was being here reminding me of what could happen in a small plane in a continent like Africa, it also brought back vivid memories of Roger that day.

I looked at the stump of my leg which marked the biggest difference between the two take-offs and told Mummbar, "Nothing's written in stone. Life's like that. What happened to Peter wasn't your fault, nor was the accident. Taking everything into account, I've got to be grateful that I'm alive. But I'll tell you one thing: the bastards who killed Peter are going to pay for what they did. I don't care how long it takes. I'm determined to see that through."

Mummbar nodded and looked away as the pilot told us to fasten our seat belts. I closed my eyes and as the plane taxied into take-off position, I prayed in silence. The roar of the engine was bringing it all back and I could feel a film of cold sweat forming on my forehead.

Once in the air, a few minutes later, I slowly reopened my eyes, and the tension started to leave my tense muscles. I gulped some cool air in, and let my eye run over the vastness of the savanna below me, and the old fascination worked its charm on me and I relaxed completely. For a few minutes I avoided eye contact with Mummbar, who seemed to have sensed what I was going through. "Relax, John. There's nothing to worry about."

I just nodded, preferring to work on my mood, knowing that any reference to what had happened or about how safe everything was now, was only going to bring the whole thing back with a rush.

A few hours later, after crossing a great chunk of Tanzania, we landed at the same airport where we had all arrived at, almost four months before. It seemed more like a lifetime before. Almost everything had changed. Peter was dead, Mike was already back in England, and I'd been changed forever. It was hard to believe that all that had happened, in a little less than four months.

I gathered my crutches together and got down onto the tarmac, breathing deeply, noting a vehicle parked near the plane. The driver put it into gear and drove over and parked in front of us. "Mister Mummbar," he said, leaning out the window, smiling.

"Good afternoon, Samson," Mummbar said, as I recognized the driver as the man who had taken us to the hotel that day.

"It's great to see you again," Samson said. "I heard there'd been some problems. I hope they'll all be fixed soon."

"Thanks, Samson. That's exactly what we want," Mummbar agreed.

Samson took a quick look at me, and then threw my bag into the car. "Get in young fellow," he said, taking my crutches from me and waiting for me to slide across the seat, before he accommodated the crutches at my side.

All the way, Samson didn't stop asking Mummbar questions about what was happening on the Reserve.

"Do you know why he's called Samson?" Mummbar asked me during the drive, looking at the two dark brown eyes of the driver, looking at us through the rear vision mirror.

"No, why?" I asked, shaking my head.

"My friend is a Masai, a true warrior, he was a Moran. And once, in his youth, he fought a lion who was threatening his younger brother."

"And?" I asked incredulously.

"He wounded the lion."

Samson interrupted him, putting the facts straight. "I killed him with my bare hands."

"That's incredible," I said.

Mummbar took over again. "A Masai warrior or Moran only hunts to show his courage, never to eat. That's why they say that God created this tribe first, then the man, and later the cattle, so they'd live together."

"What Mister Mummbar is telling you is true," Samson said.

"That's why all the cattle in the world are considered theirs by divine right," Mummbar went on. "They were sent by God to predict the future and attract rain where there wasn't any. According to them, they are the lost tribe of Judah. And on top of all that, my friend Samson is a hero. That's why he's got five wives, no less! Isn't that right, Samson? Or am I mistaken?"

Samson explained as he drove on, that he'd decided a few years before to dedicate himself to only one of the wives. He'd become a Christian and renounced polygamy. Until the arrival in his village of Christian preachers, those few years before he'd followed the rites of Engai, the god of the sky and provider of cattle. But that was now a thing of the past.

"I'm completely faithful to Jecinta," he informed us, swerving sharply to avoid a street vendor, who cursed us as we sped on.

I looked at the man through the rear window. He was carrying ivory ornaments and ebony masks and had only just managed to keep his balance. He continued to throw abuse at us, as Samson wound the window down and poked his head out. "What do you expect if you walk the streets like a dog!"

The incident reminded me of my first impression of Samson four months before. He wasn't easily intimidated, and always gave back more than he received.

A bit further on, on the periphery of Dar es Salaam,

we came across an accident at one of the intersections that had created a traffic jam, which kept us bogged down for hours, and finally forced us to make a detour. I was looking at my watch constantly, worrying that I'd miss my flight home. And to make things worse, we ran into a street market further on, with hundreds of salesmen weaving their way through the traffic. One group of vendors, some Hindus, speaking in an almost incomprehensible English, offered us a young girl. I wound the window down in disgust, as they continued to harass us along the street.

We eventually got moving again but hadn't driven much more than another ten minutes, when a raggedly dressed man, winding his way across the street, almost crashed into us. I stared at him in shock as he weaved around us and continued on his way. I opened the door to the car, dragging my crutches after me and got out as quickly as I could, hell-bent on following this mysterious vagabond who was disappearing into a sea of people. "I'll catch up with you in a few minutes." I called back to a shocked Mummbar, who no doubt thought I'd lost my mind.

Desperately, I went off in the direction the man had gone, worried that I'd lost contact with him, but a few seconds later, I saw him stop beside the door of a foul-smelling tavern, where he lay down against the wall. I hobbled over to him as quickly as I could, my heart thumping in my chest, leaned over and he looked up at me angrily, and when I saw his face and confirmed my suspicions, I just stood there in the street, propping myself up, more shocked than I'd ever been in my life.

CHAPTER
TWENTY-EIGHT

On observing that almost lifeless face, with its lost look and great scar above the eyebrow that ran to the edge of his temple, I bent down and took his hands in mine.

"Peter, Pete!" I said incredulously, doubly shocked to find him alive and in the condition he was in.

"Peter, Pete? Who's that?" he said, suddenly frightened, pulling his hands away from mine. "I don't know what you're talking about, sir. I don't know you."

"But, Pete! What are you saying? I'm John... John Carmichael, your friend."

"I don't know anyone called John," he said angrily, shaking his head. "And I've never seen you before."

It was obvious that he'd been badly beaten and was suffering from amnesia.

Samson pulled the van up beside us and Mummbar got out quickly. He had the same shocked expression on his face that I'd had minutes before. And reached out and restrained Peter as he tried to make a bolt for it.

"Let me go! Let me go!" he yelled, while he was being held, without anybody in the surrounding crowd showing the least interest in him or us.

"Calm down, man," Mummbar shouted. "We're your friends and here to help you, and take you home to your wife, Claire."

"Claire? Claire?" he said, seemingly stunned by the mention of the name. "I've heard that name before."

"That's it, Peter. Claire, she's the mother of your child," Mummbar said.

"You see," I said, as Samson opened the rear door with a strange look on his face, visibly confused by what was happening. "I'm going to take you home to Claire."

Once inside the van, he said nothing more, and just sat there like a sack of rocks, mumbling the name Peter over and over again. He was finding it difficult to breathe, his expression lost.

"That's it, mate," I said, taking his passport out of the briefcase and showing it to him.

He squinted, trying to focus on the photo, examining it in detail, running his hands over his own face, desperately. It was obvious that his tortured, drug-affected mind, couldn't come to terms with what some isolated part of his memory was telling him was true.

"Don't stress yourself out, Pete. When you're back home with your family, it'll all come back," I said patting him on the shoulder.

His hands lay limply on his legs, and overwhelmed by whatever drugs were in his system, by fear, and the confusion of what was happening to him, he began to cry.

A few minutes before arriving at the airport, Mummbar ordered Samson to stop at a motel, about a half a block from where we were, as he glanced at his watch. "We've got fifteen minutes at the most to give him a bath. We can't take him to the airport like this. He needs a change of clothes; he looks like a street bum."

With Samson's help, Mummbar got a protesting Peter out of the car, while I went to the reception, and explained that we needed a room for a few minutes, while the receptionist, aghast at the site of the man who was going to occupy one of his rooms, upped the price immediately.

"Okay, I'll pay the difference," I told him. "We're in a hurry, give me the keys!"

With a look of disgust on his face, he finally relented and gave me the keys. "Room seven, down the steps at the end of the corridor, but the money first."

As I was paying him, Mummbar and Samson rushed Peter down the corridor and into the room. They had his clothes off before he knew what was happening, the foul stench of his body filling the small motel room. It was clear he hadn't had a shower since he'd left Gambala. And we were shocked to see the signs of torture that were evident on his naked body. There were scars and burns and bruises all over his chest and back.

"John, I'll go and get some clean clothes from the bag. I'll throw these filthy rags he's been wearing away," Mummbar said, leaving the room, as Samson turned the shower on, and then somehow managed to get Peter under the jet of water as he struggled, grunting like a wild animal. The cold water did nothing to soothe his scarred and painful body.

"Sorry I've got to put you through this, Mister," Samson said coughing, battling against the stench around him. "But it's got to be better for you to be clean. And it certainly is for us."

We ignored his groans, and when the ordeal was

over, Mummbar was waiting at the door with a towel. We dressed and tidied him up the best that we could, and noticed that he seemed a little more lucid than he had been before. No doubt the effect of the drugs was receding in his body.

We eventually arrived at the airport with time to spare, while Mummbar went off to buy Peter's ticket, ensuring that he was next to me, as well as organizing a wheel chair to get Peter onto the plane. "I'll be back soon," I told Mummbar when he came back and we finally separated. It was a moving farewell because he'd been so good to me in the last few months, helping to get me motivated again.

"Take care, John, we'll miss you," was all he could say, hugging me like a father would his son, visibly touched by having to say goodbye.

I watched him go, a tall figure cutting his way through the crowd and realized I was on my own now. And turning back, I noticed a lot of the other passengers staring at Peter. "Haven't you ever seen a sick person before," I said, my tired and irritated voice surprising both them and myself.

They looked away, more than one of them red-faced, and a short while later, an assistant pushed Peter in the wheel chair to the plane, then helped him walk up the stairs, and with his hand around his arm assisted him to his seat. It all must have been too much for Peter because by the time his safety belt was fastened, he was fast asleep, and looking haggard, under a mane of unruly hair and wild beard that covered his cracked lips, making him look like a homeless destitute.

CHAPTER
TWENTY-NINE

On returning to London I went straight to Gwyn's house to collect old Morris. I'd got used to people looking at me on crutches, staring at the space where my leg had once been, but it was hard to see my sister, trying her best not to show her shock. I tried to talk as if everything was just as it had been when I left, telling her about the wonder of Africa, as well as the down side of my trip there. But in the end it was all too much for her and she broke down and cried uncontrollably on hearing what had happened to me on the savanna after the crash.

Peter had been placed in a rehabilitation clinic and was making slow progress in regaining his ravaged memory, with Claire at his side, and his one-month-old son, Christopher, putting a smile on his face now and again. But he still didn't know who I was, even though I visited him almost every day.

I'd only spoken to Mike twice by telephone since I'd returned and decided on the spur of the moment one night, to visit him in his plush apartment a few blocks from King's Road. I rang the bronze bell, and was surprised to find him with a guitar in his hand when he opened the door. He led me down the corridor to the dining room decorated in retro style, where on the walls five enormous modernist paintings of the Beatles were hanging.

"Five," I wondered, running my eye over the faces on the wall, and began to laugh when I saw Mike's face hanging up there with John, Paul, Ringo and George.

"You're the only one who's noticed me there," Mike said. "Most of the others don't even look at the wall. It was Sarah's idea. You know she's even more eccentric than I am."

We sat down at a table and he poured us two bourbons on the rocks, while we talked about the trip. We had a few laughs talking about the funnier moments of that African odyssey, but it didn't take him too long to get back to the dark side of our time there.

"I can tell you, John, I never thought you were going to come out of that coma. But look at you now, you look great! You've got that old look back in your eye. It must be Marie. You've got no idea what she did for you when you were in that hospital. It sort of made your condition seem even worse with her sitting there, day after day, waiting for you to wake up. It's a pity you're not with her now."

"I know," I said taking a slow sip of the bourbon. "But I hope it won't be for long. As soon as we've done what we have to do here, and we've taken these corrupt bastards apart. I'll go back and live there."

Mike looked astonished by what I'd just said.

"Seriously? After all that happened, you'd give everything up here to go and live in Gambala?"

I shrugged my shoulders and raised my eyebrows. "Life's complicated, Mike. You know that."

"But it's a big change. You must be head over heels in love with the French woman to even consider it."

"Which French woman are we talking about? I'm getting a little jealous," Sarah said, walking into the room, carrying a bag of rag paper in her arms. She was pallid, had dark rings under her eyes, and didn't look well at all.

"Marie, the French doctor I told you about who fell for John's charms," Mike said, getting up to greet her.

"Hi Sarah, how are you?" I said, struggling to get up, too.

"John," she said, stopping me with her hand. "I'm better, but... I can't believe it. Mike told me what happened. You don't know how sorry I was to hear about your accident."

I was getting used to these sorts of reactions. After having seen me during all our relationship with two legs, it was a shock now to see me with one. "But thank God you're alive. And you're back here, and as handsome as ever," she said, with a light smile on her white face. "Well, boys, I'll leave the two of you to it. I guess you've got a lot to talk about."

She kissed me on the cheek and told Mike that Charles Myers from *Geo World* had phoned to inform him that they were ready to erect the daises in the park.

"I've been busy the last month, John," Mike confided in me after his wife had left the room. "We should be able to take our first steps against McMahon and Dormonth now."

He explained his progress with the editors and

publishers of *Geo World* during the last two months, and one of them, the Charles Myers that Sarah had said had rung, had been compiling information and putting everything in chronological order: photographs, films, facts, editing, and was preparing a documentary that was almost finished, taking into account every detail of our investigation. It was clear from what Mike was telling me that the finished product was going to be very professional and controversial. It would last an hour and be presented under the theme of the community fight against environmental malpractice, of the struggle of environmentalists from the European Union and world ecological groups, against the dirty tricks of UMAG and those who supported them. "It's going to create a massive backlash against what's going on there," Mike said. "Don't make any mistake about that. We're going to focus directly on the problem with Gajha, and how it's affecting the ecosystem in Tanzania and its neighboring countries. And behind all of that, John, the corruption, the socio-economic disorder will be as clear as a bell to anyone who's watching the documentary. What this program is going to do is take the lid off the whole dirty business and let the whole world look in and be duly shocked. I've taken the liberty of calling our project 'United Friends for Tanzania.' What do you think?"

"Sounds great," I said, thinking about the amount of work that must have gone into it.

"Well, listen to this, mate," Mike said, with a great enthusiastic grin on his face. "Ecofriends and Amnesty International have indicated that they'll join in. Both of them are active in the United Nations, and as you know, the minute they get involved things start happening. It will only be a question of time before this impacts on the government of Cofy Mangandi, and exerts significant socio-economic pressure on Tanzania. The whole thing's been done in a way that we've got the right proof to back up each of the individual claims."

I took another sip of the bourbon and looked at the Beatles hanging on the wall and wondered what they would've done to help if the group had still been around. And thinking that, I realized the power of the media, and the reach this documentary would have with the support of the powerful groups that Mike had just detailed.

"There'll be an exhibition and a conference, sponsored by *Geo World* in Hyde Park at the beginning of next month," Mike informed me. "There'll be giant screens everywhere, shots of the mine, of the hundreds of dead animals there, as well as in Lake Victoria. The reason for their deaths will be explained by experts. And the human problem will be highlighted. And just in case you think I've forgotten something, Interpol's helping in an investigation into the background of McMahon and Dormonth."

"Have you found anything useful yet?"

"No, not yet, John, but something's bound to turn up soon. And now that Peter's back, I've informed the media about this outrage perpetrated against him by the Tanzanian Government and a few days ago, our own government's joined the party. Reports about what happened are starting to appear on radio and TV and also in the papers. There was an article this morning, did you read it?"

"No, I still haven't got back into my old routine."

I took the opportunity then of telling Mike about my suspicions about Phillipe, asking him to have him included on Interpol's search list, about his connection to UMAG and his true intentions at Gambala.

"No problem," he said. "But that's surprising news,

I must say. But enough's enough. Tell me a little about yourself?"

"I had an appointment this morning with an orthopedic technician. I'm hoping to have a prosthesis as soon as possible."

"That's wonderful news. You're a real fighter, John. There's no doubt about that. Not everyone's got your willpower," he said, slapping me on the back.

"Well, if I don't get out there and make an effort, no one else will. It's not easy to go through life like a flamingo," I said, surprising myself with a joke at my own expense.

Mike chuckled. "I'm proud to have a friend like you, John."

I nodded. "Thanks, mate, but getting back to the other matter. What worries me about all this publicity is that maybe we're going to see some reprisals. Even though everything's been presented exactly as it is, I've got to ask myself what the vested interests back there are going to do about this. I'm only saying this because we've got to be prepared for what's likely to come out of this."

"Yes, I know that," Mike agreed. "But there's no backing out now. What they did to Peter is unacceptable. We were sitting around here for months thinking he was dead. It was an extraordinary stroke of luck you had in finding him when you did. Another few months living the way he was, he probably would've died. And we would have been none the wiser."

"You're not wrong there," I said. "Sometimes I have to ask myself why things like that happen. The chances of finding a needle in a haystack aren't high you know."

It'd been great to see Mike again and listen to his report. It lifted my hopes a lot higher that sooner or later, justice would prevail, and that those responsible would finish up behind bars.

I collected my crutches, got up and made my way to the front door. "Careful, John, I don't want to see you fall over and dent your pride."

"Don't worry, mate. It's hard to get up and not easy to walk, but I haven't lost the plot like you have, in proclaiming yourself the fifth Beatle."

I could hear him laughing behind me. "You've got a point there, John."

I hailed the first taxi that came down the street and arranged to meet Mike the next day to visit Peter together. The thought of that took the smile off my face as I drove away. I couldn't see Pete getting out of the clinic any time soon.

CHAPTER
THIRTY

The following morning, as we'd arranged, Mike passed by to collect me on his way to visit Peter. He was carrying a complete album of photographs of our trip to Tanzania, which was the first thing I noticed when I got in the car.

"I thought the photos and the three of us together might help him remember something," he explained as we pulled out into the traffic. "We've got to find a way of touching a nerve somewhere. And we both know that photographs are a powerful tool. Even if he only remembers one, it's a step in the right direction."

I was thinking about what Mike had just said as we drove past Buckingham Palace, and watched a demonstration of Liberal Democrats outside. "We'll be doing that in a few days."

"No, John. We're going much higher than that. Tanzania's a long way away, my friend. A simple march or a strike won't be enough to get our message across."

"That's true, enough," I agreed, thinking about all the different plans of action that Mike had already outlined, as the car turned the corner and we pulled up in front of the hospital.

I had the same nervous feeling in the pit of my stomach that I'd had ever since I'd first realized that Pete had lost his memory. It's something we all take for granted, but not being able to remember what happened yesterday or a year ago, or five years before that, wipes out an individual's personality. All the bits that went into making Pete who he was: the memories of his childhood, his marriage, his work, were in effect, lost. If just a little bit of that could be found, maybe the rest would follow suit. At least, that was what I was thinking as we walked down the long corridor to his room.

We knocked a few times, but when there was no answer, we opened the door. Peter was alone, sitting on a wheel chair at the window, staring as if hypnotized at other patients walking in the garden outside.

"Pete!" I said as we closed the door behind us, trying to let him know that we were in the room.

"How are you, mate?" Mike asked walking up to him.

There was no expression on his face, and he hardly turned to welcome us. "Well, I guess," he said turning the wheel chair around to look at us. "I don't remember anything. Or that close enough to nothing that it's more or less the same thing. I know you're my friends because Claire's told me about you. And besides, you wouldn't come here every day if you weren't." He watched us sit down on the edge of the bed. "I remember Claire, though. But strangely it doesn't go any further than that."

"No one else?" I asked, leaning forward towards him.

"In the last few days, a black face has been muscling its way into my dreams. He's more or less there every night, and as far as I can make out, his name is Captain something. But I'm not sure, it's all very hazy."

Mike and I moved closer, I opened the photo album and put it on the blanket on his knees. "Sounds like Captain Mbongo to me." To which Peter only shrugged his shoulders.

"Take a look at the photos in this album," Mike encouraged him. "You might remember someone."

Pete started turning the pages slowly, and almost straight away, he seemed to be in the grip of his emotions, as his hands left the album and started rubbing his forehead.

"What's wrong, Pete?" I asked him. "Do you recognize someone?"

He didn't even seem to hear me, his whole body shaking, mumbling to himself. He seemed to be having some sort of fit, when Mike jumped to his feet and took a firm hold of his shoulders.

"We're here, Pete. You're not alone! If something's scratched your memory that's all right, more than all right."

Peter's eyes were only half open, but they seemed to be looking everywhere around him as if the room was suddenly full of ghosts. I had the impression that something in the album had unlocked a gate, and a whole host of memories were charging in. I dragged myself up on my crutches, went to the door, and as I was about to call for a nurse, Peter stopped me, "Wait, John!" he said, calling me by my name for the first time since he'd been taken away that day in Gambala.

I turned around, and looked at the stunned expression on Mike's face, standing behind him.

"Something's coming back," Peter said. "Though

it's like looking at a parade coming down the street, you don't know what's coming next. I can see the three of us in Africa and things started falling apart when…" he closed his eyes as if that was going to help him bring it all back. "When those supposed officials came to the ranch, I can remember them talking about a place called Dodoma. I think my eyes were taped. They locked me in a room that stank of manure and I could hear the sound of animals. I was hungry, yes, I can remember that. Very hungry! But they gave me some foul smelling water to drink and forced me to drink it. And after that I became delirious. I'm sure they gave me some sort of drug to get me to confess. They wanted me to tell the truth. But I didn't know what truth they were talking about. Yes, that's how it was. My nightmare began in that room."

Mike took his hands off Pete's shoulders, while I stood in front of him, leaning on my crutches, astonished at the sudden retrieval of his memory.

"And what happened then, mate?" Mike asked, lowering his head.

Peter took his time to answer, rubbing his forehead again, trying to put everything in sequence. "I think I was tied to a metal chair, with my eyes still taped, until one day they ripped the tape off, and I was half blinded by the light. I sort of remember a white man being there. But I didn't recognize him. All I remember then is them beating me. Grabbing me by the shirt and beating me, over and over again, until I was almost unconscious. After that, they kept asking me questions about the mine and our relation with someone called Turman and another name I don't remember."

"You mean, Turner, don't you? And the other man would've been Mummbar. Do you remember that name?"

"I don't know, maybe. I just remember that they wanted me to confess, to what according to them, I had seen at the airfield or something like that. I don't remember saying anything then and they beat me. I came to the conclusion that it didn't matter what I said or didn't say, they were going to kill me anyway."

"And then what?" I asked.

"Take it easy, John," Mike advised me. "Don't rush him. Let him take his time."

"I'm sorry, Pete," I said, realizing that Mike was right.

"There's a lot in my head that I just don't understand," Pete explained.

"They tortured me physically and mentally. They'd push me to the limit, and just when I thought it was all over, they'd start again.

"They'd keep me awake, and not ask me anything for a while and then the interrogation would start once more. I remember my head being pushed into a tub of frozen water. And…" He stopped talking, as if whatever it was that he was about to tell us was too terrible to put into words.

"What's wrong, mate?" Mike asked, resting his hand on his arm again.

"I did a terrible thing," he said, his face contorted in revulsion.

I tried to calm him down. "Take your time, Pete. Nice and slow."

He took my advice and then went on. "At some point in all of this, with my hands still tied behind my back, I threw myself at one of them and ripped a part of his ear off with my teeth."

The shock of reliving that made him close his eyes again, trying to get around that, before he revealed any more details of the living nightmare he'd been through.

It was clearer now than it had been before, why Peter's mind had simply shut down. There had to be some system of self protection working there.

He opened his eyes and went on. "After that, I remember them mentioning someone called McMahon a few times, when suddenly, I felt a really heavy blow to my head, and don't remember anything else until I woke up one morning not far from where you found me. I had no idea who or where I was. I most probably would have died, but a young man found me in a metal pipe where they throw toxic waste, a few miles from Dar es Salaam. I guess you could say he saved my life. I don't know how long I'd been there, but the man who pulled me out, told me that half of my body had been floating in a phosphorescent, violet-coloured liquid. I found out, soon enough after I got out of there, that my legs and arms were covered in sores with black holes in them," he said, stretching his arms out to show veins that were still bruised.

I wasn't too sure if he really wanted to go on talking, there was nothing but pain in all these memories. But they were his reality, and he needed to get it off his chest.

"On top of that foul liquid that they made me drink, they must have injected me with something. And in the middle of my delirium and confusion, the man who found me gave me some narcotics to ease the pain. Without that and the food he brought me, I would have been long gone. It was terrible. My body kept demanding more and more drugs to keep me afloat. I was completely mad."

"What else did you hear about McMahon? He was the bloke at the mine who told us about the gold extraction process, remember?" Mike asked him.

"I told you it's not easy remembering anything clearly. I never saw anyone during all that time. I just know he was there because I heard him answer to his name. And I know for certain that he was one of the leaders, because on one of the days that they moved me, the rest of them were giving him a report about what had been going on. And there was somebody else there, too. They called him the Boss."

"It's pretty clear that McMahon and Dormonth, and maybe Kassam Mangandi, have been in on all of this from the beginning. They started this, now it's up to us to finish it," I said angrily.

Peter started turning the pages of the album again. Something, one of the photos there, or time itself, had switched on a light in his head, as he looked at each image grimly from the bunker of a new depression.

Sadness has many faces, and even though it was terrible to see him the way he had been, unable to remember even the most basic things from the past, his face was more painfully expressive now, and that made me feel so sorry for him.

"This is the man who appears night after night in my dreams!" Pete said, pointing at Captain Mbongo standing next to his wife. "He was worried about me and gave me a revolver to defend myself with."

"He's a good man," Mike explained, telling Peter about the ranch and what had gone on there. "He's involved in this project with us. He's one of the United Friends for Tanzania."

Peter looked at the stump of my leg for the first time in all those weeks. "And what happened to you, John?"

"I had a fight with a lion, but as you can see, I wasn't as tough as I thought I was," I said, smiling. "But that's another story. Let's leave it for another day. You've been through a lot in the last hour. And I've got to go."

"Are you sure, John?" Mike asked. "I can give you a lift home."

"No thanks, after this conversation, a little walk won't hurt me, although I'm not likely to get very far," I said, patting Pete on the back as I made my way to the door.

"Take care, John. I'll see you later," Mike called after me on my way to the door, as Claire arrived with a bunch of flowers in her hand. I kissed her on the cheek, and continued on my way, past a group of nurses huddled around a swarthy foreigner, who was screaming so loudly in his own language that for a second I tried to cover my ears with my hands, as a little girl charged through the door to the clinic, crashing into me and sending me flying. I hit the ground hard at the feet of one of the security men standing at the door.

"I'm so sorry, sir," the little girl said, rushing over to me, and helping me to sit up.

"Don't worry about it," I said, rubbing my knee. "It happens all the time."

"Sophie, what happened?" a soft feminine voice behind me asked.

"I ran into this man and knocked him over."

"I'm very sorry," the voice with a trace of a French accent said. "She runs everywhere without looking where she's going."

The security guard and the girl's mother helped me to my feet, but when the woman, who'd been behind me, saw my face, she gasped. "John!"

I was still struggling with my crutches when she said my name, and staring into her eyes, I was shocked to see who it was.

CHAPTER
THIRTY-ONE

I kept staring into those bright green eyes that were suddenly carrying me back across the vast savanna of time. A lump forming in my throat as I flew, a stab of guilt found, on landing. "Jackie? What are you doing here?"

"I could ask you the same question," she replied, her eyes discreetly finding the space where my leg had once been. "What happened to you, John?"

"It's a long story, cut short," I said trying to be funny.

"Dear God, John. I'm so sorry!"

"That makes two of us," I said, taking my crutches and making my way to the door to get away from the crowd inside the clinic looking at us. Jackie and her daughter followed me.

"Her daughter?" I whispered to myself, as I leant on a drink machine outside. And looking back, I stared at the little girl, around nine years old, who was walking towards me. She had the same green eyes as her mother, light brown hair and freckles scattered across her nose and cheeks.

She was obviously worried about me. "Is something wrong, sir? Do you feel all right? Don't you think it would be better to sit down for a while before you leave?"

"No, dear, I'm fine. Thanks for the thought, just the same," I said, looking back at Jackie, who looked as serious as I felt.

"Really, what are you doing here, John?" she asked me.

"I came to visit Peter. Maybe you remember him. He was a friend at the university."

She nodded her head slowly. "I think so. Wasn't he Claire Spotiswoode's boyfriend?"

"That's him, they're married now. But unfortunately he's here, in the clinic. Don't ask me why, because it's another long story. And you?" I asked, looking at her daughter Sophie half of the time.

"I work here, John. I specialize in neuro-traumatology. My office is two blocks from here, but I've been in charge of rehabilitation in the clinic for the last six years."

"Congratulations, Jackie. And you're still as beautiful as ever," I said, noting the ring on her finger, which stirred my curiosity. "Did you get married?"

"Yes, I married a wonderful man, Sophie's father," she said with the hint of a stutter.

My curiosity was more than stirred, now it was rampant, and with little Sophie's presence there were playing a game of cat and mouse.

"And do you have any other children?"

But Sophie answered this time. "No, I'm an only child, but you two seem to have known each other for a long time, isn't that right?"

"That's right, sweetheart, " her mother said, putting her hand out and shaking mine. "Well, I'm afraid I've got to go. It's been nice seeing you again after such a long time. I hope you can get some help with the mobility in your leg, John. If you need anything don't hesitate to call."

"Thanks," I said, leaning forward and kissing her involuntarily on the cheek and Sophie on the head. I sensed this was the little girl who had been following me all those years in my dreams, asking me why?

I left the hospital wondering if I would ever see them again, and if life was going to give me a chance to mend the great error I'd made in my youth. I felt suddenly empty inside, a feeling that didn't go away in the next few days, as I secluded myself in my flat, and silently plunged the depths of depression.

CHAPTER
THIRTY-TWO

After more than a week of living like a hermit with Morris the Faithful at my side, I rekindled enough energy to face the world again. I knew there wasn't much point moping around my flat for another week, going over and over something that couldn't be undone. But regardless of that, I'd still needed to lock myself away for a while, even though I knew there wasn't much point in the exercise.

In the depths of my deep reflection during those days, I remembered one of the Beatles, John Lennon, no doubt prompted by having seen his face on Mike's living room wall a few days before. He'd locked himself away, too, for different reasons, but sometimes for years. Maybe it was that, that finally pushed me out into the fog and rain again.

I visited an orthopedic surgeon my first day out, which showed I meant business. I wanted to get back on two legs again. To get moving and avoid those constant looks of pity that hurt me, more than anything else, in the maelstrom of change that losing a leg implies.

I went back to the clinic to visit Peter, and hopefully see Jackie, too. I needed to talk to her. To hear her say that her life was a dream now and that she'd forgiven me completely for what had happened all those years before. But I kept on imagining her slamming the door in my face, which I figured she had every right to do.

As soon as I got into the entrance hall, I headed straight to the lifts, past what seemed like dozens of patients, wandering around, carrying plastic drip bags held on metal supports. The rehabilitation wing was at the end of the corridor, so I made my way there, and to a small window behind which a young nurse was sitting, looking bored with a telephone in her hand.

"Excuse me," I said in little more than a whisper. "Would Doctor Jackie Guirmand be on duty today?"

She covered the receiver with her hand and asked: "And your name is?"

I felt suddenly nervous and had the feeling I shouldn't be there. "John Carmichael."

"Wait a second," she said, pressing a number on the panel beside the phone. "There's a John Carmichael here to see you."

I walked away from the window and looked at my watch a couple of times for something to do, before Jackie came through a door at the end of the room with a stethoscope around her neck. She looked absolutely self assured as she walked up to me. "What can I do for you, John? I'm very busy today."

It wasn't exactly the sort of reception I'd been hoping for, and made me feel all the more nervous. "I'm sorry to bother you here at the clinic. But it was nice to see you the other day and…, well I thought maybe you could find the time to have a cup of coffee with me."

Her left eyebrow arched, as she took me by the elbow and led me back to the corridor. "And what have you and I got to talk about, John? It was all perfectly clear enough ten years ago, don't you think? What's the point of talking about all of that again? You chose to get on with your life without any encumbrances, and I chose to enjoy the greatest treasure there is in the world. But let me tell you, that in all that time, I've never stopped thanking God for having made the best decision in my life."

I wasn't sure what I should say to that but tried. "I admire you, Jackie. And although you probably don't believe me, I regretted what I did. I looked for you everywhere, but it was like you just disappeared from the face of the earth."

She interrupted me. "This is not the time or the place to talk about that, John. I've got people waiting for me."

"Yes, of course. But I would like the chance to speak to you, though," I said, taking out a business card and giving it to her.

She frowned, looked at it for a few seconds and then put it in a pocket of her white coat. "See you around, John," she said, kissing me on the cheek before going back through the door she'd entered from.

I felt like a complete idiot, as I made my way to Peter's room, going over what she'd said, and my own miserable words.

Claire and her sister were there when I opened the door.

"Peter's in one of his therapies, John. He could be there for another forty minutes. Do you want to wait?" she said standing up.

I shook my head, turning back to the door. "I'm sorry. It's not one of my better days. Just tell Pete that I came to visit him. And that Mike and I are going ahead with everything we told him the other day. I'll pop in to see him in the next few days."

She half nodded, with an understanding look on her face, as if she'd been privy to what had taken place downstairs a few minutes before. "Sure, John, I'll tell him."

Three weeks went by with constant visits to the orthopedic technician. He kept on doing tests and adjusting the prosthesis that would replace a third of my leg. It was difficult to learn how to control it and also to accept it as being part of me. But the hope of walking without relying on crutches was a big incentive. With good therapy and the right attitude, I was able to throw the crutches away and replace them with an elegant silver-handled walking stick that Gwyn bought me on a trip to Paris. I got to use it for the first time, the day of the conference in Hyde Park.

I drove my black Volvo there that day. It had been parked in front of my building for a few months and, in a way, being behind the wheel, driving down London's magnificent streets, was a symbol of me being back. I felt better than I had since things had turned bad in Gambala, excited that my recovery and the fruition of our efforts had come together at the same time.

I missed Marie terribly, and imagined how much she would have enjoyed this day in the park, because in many ways, of all the activists involved, she was the most dedicated.

I parked my car a few blocks away in Knightsbridge, walked to the park gates and a few minutes later reached one of the daises, surrounded by gigantic loudspeakers, screens and spectacular billboards, which displayed many of the photographs that we'd taken during our trip there. I looked straight away at me holding little Nina in my arms, and everything came storming so vividly back.

I found Mike and Charles from *Geo World* in a campaign tent beside the platform where they were going over the details of the presentation with a small group of people. It seemed to me that Mike hadn't forgotten anything, but there was a lot to show the building crowd outside and he wanted everything, particularly the sequence of presentations to run smoothly.

At five o'clock the event got underway, in front of a vast crowd that had formed on an open space in the park. There were people from all over England there, along with tourists of every race and colour. It was something to see, and I felt a sense of pride and satisfaction that we had been capable of putting it all together in such a relatively short time.

The six exhibitors, including myself, went up on stage and sat at a table, while Mike started the proceedings. He explained the devastation that had occurred and the role of the mines in that, while his words were backed up with images on the screens around us. The crowd looked on in silence at the scenes of dead animals lying everywhere around Urekewe, at the resulting impact on the towns, and at photos of what had happened in Sector 38 at Gajha. It was easy to see that all of that affected the crowd, and by the time Mike had finished his report, the faces that greeted me as I took the microphone had changed. It was a captive, concerned throng now, as I explained our goals and the dedication of Gambala to saving the wildlife in the north of Tanzania.

We showed a film which started with me rescuing Nina that day by the lake, her arrival at the Reserve and her subsequent recovery. But she was only one of dozens of animals presented, featuring the care taken in their rehabilitation and their subsequent release back into the wild.

I turned many times during my speech to talk about various scenes on the great screen behind me, where more often than not, Marie was seen going about her work. I almost had the feeling that she was really there, as I continued to speak about the urgency of the situation in Gambala, and the undoubted fate of the animal population there, if the pollution wasn't stopped now!

A representative of Amnesty International, Ian Shiffer, took over after me, detailing what had happened to Thabo, Galijha, Gatto and Peter, as well as talking about the millions of people around the world who were victims of human rights violations. He emphasized the role of big business in all of this and the forming of powerful corrupt labour unions who were nearly as much to blame as the companies themselves in those countries where abuses were perpetrated. And almost an hour and a half after we had started, Charles summed up with a special sentence dedicated to those responsible. "The greed for gold, that has bathed its brilliant colour in blood, will soon come to an end."

We all stood up and thanked the thousands of people present for having found the time to come and listen to our cause. And judging by the crowd's reaction, it seemed we'd got off to a good start.

We went to Charles house in the elegant suburb of Belgravia after Hyde Park, where we sipped cocktails and ate exotic hors d'oeuvres, while we were entertained by bagpipers and a jazz trio that played the rest of the night. It was a good way to finish what had been a very satisfying day, and a little before two in the morning, everybody started working their way home.

It was cold and foggy outside, the night sky beginning to spit rain. I did my jacket up tight and pulled the lapels high up around my neck, but the frosty wind still cut through, so I walked faster. The streets were lonely and glistening under the street lamps, and not far from Harrods, I became aware of somebody following me. I looked over my shoulder a couple of times and eventually saw a shadow pull back into an alley not far behind me. I quickened my pace even more, but around ten yards from my car, I could see that the windscreen had been smashed to bits.

I walked up to the Volvo slowly, my anger rising, as I took my keys out and opened the door. But before I could get in, a black glove grabbed my shoulder and my heart missed a beat.

CHAPTER
THIRTY-THREE

Without being able to see behind me and on the point of swinging around and giving whoever it was my best right-hand punch, a deep voice asked me. "Are you all right, sir?"

To my relief, I turned to find a policeman behind me, carrying a powerful hand torch.

"I can't say that I do feel all that well to come back here and find my car like this, " I said, showing him the front seat covered in glass. "And as far as I can make out up to now, whoever did this, has stolen a folder with very important information in it."

He asked me for the car's papers and my identification and started filling out some paperwork to file a report back at the police station, which we went to when he was finished.

It was five in the morning when I finally got home and staggered to my desk. I was lucky that the papers that were stolen were copies and not the originals that

Mike kept in his flat. That was something to be grateful for, but the question that kept doing the rounds in my head was, who could have broken into my car, and why?

I sat down behind the desk, opened the top drawer, and took out the photo I'd taken of Marie shortly before my return to London, and put it into a silver frame that my parents had given me. Marie looked even better set against the silver, and even though I needed to sleep, a great urge to write her a letter came over me.

I gave her a progress report, telling her about the success of the exhibition at Hyde Park, of Peter's improvement, and finished up by telling her how much I loved and missed her. And even though it made me feel better to have put pen to paper, it still didn't make getting to sleep any easier, as I tossed and turned, with birds chirping in the early morning light outside the window. A great day had finished badly and I couldn't help wondering, if this was just the beginning of something we hadn't bargained for?

A few weeks passed, with follow up interviews, and conferences, and a television debate, in which new proposals were put forward to fix the environmental damage in Africa. Although Gajha was our priority, it wasn't the only mine, or indeed industry, involved in the polluting of Africa. There were plenty more scattered around the shores of Urekewe. It was a heated television debate, because we faced three mining entrepreneurs, one from Canada, a Peruvian and an Argentinean, who interrupted everyone when they were speaking and wouldn't shut up when it was his turn to put his point of view across. He tried to convince the viewing public that we had inflated the whole thing out of proportion. And while that was frustrating and incorrect, it still brought the subject to the public's attention which was really our main objective.

After several months of traveling and more public presentations in search of international support, our efforts started to bear fruit around the world. The mine at Punta Peñasco in South America, one of the most famous in the world, was closed after twenty years of causing devastating pollution around the mine, and causing the indiscriminate death of cattle and multimillion dollar losses to their owners. Also, many countries sensitive to environmental issues were motivated by the increased publicity that we had managed to create to increase government controls and implement measures that indirectly resulted in the closure of many mines and the affective censuring of others. Quality controls were introduced and pollution, as a result, was significantly reduced. All of that pointed to the success of our tactics, but unfortunately, Gajha remained one of those mines where nothing had changed.

The stumbling block was the Tanzanian government itself, which simply ignored the issue. And without feeling personally offended by the images that had been shown to have taken place in their country, it was obvious that some other, stronger measure was required.

On one of those nights, after a day of intense activity, we decided to celebrate the fact that Peter had been released from the clinic, after four months of rehabilitation, and exactly seven long months after he'd been taken prisoner at Gambala. Mike and I took him to the King's Horseman Pub, where we'd used to meet a couple of times a month before we went to Africa.

During the first hour there, I noted that Pete seemed to be uncomfortable, looking around himself constantly, his hand shaking, as he lifted his glass to his mouth.

"What's up, Pete? You look nervous," I asked him.

"Yes, that's exactly how I feel. Somebody's watching me," he informed us.

"What are you talking about, mate?" Mike said. "Who's watching you?"

He sounded paranoid, when he answered. "A black man was watching me through that window. Don't think I'm crazy. I'm sure I'm being watched, they tried to kill me the other night at the clinic."

"What are you talking about, Pete? Are you serious?" I asked him, leaning forward.

"Deadly serious, I'm afraid. A few nights back, I woke up with a strange feeling," he said, looking back at the window. "I sensed somebody standing there at the head of the bed. I half opened my eyes and saw the silhouette of a man standing there with something in his hand. I thought it was one of the nurses, checking something, and closed my eyes again, but after a while, I reopened them again and saw a figure hiding behind one of the curtains."

I urged him to go on. "And what happened?"

"I was about to call out and ask him what he was doing, but just as I was about to do that, he stepped into the moonlight and I sensed that things weren't quite right. I was exhausted after having taken my medication and closed my eyes again, only to feel a blow to my head almost straight away and realized that somebody had covered my head with a pillow and was trying to suffocate me."

Both Mike and I were dumbfounded. "And then?" Mike asked.

"I fought like a lion. I was lucky that my hands were above the sheets, and I managed to ring the bell that was on one of the tables near my bed. The intruder must've realized that, 'cause he took off straight away."

"Did you get a look at his face?" I asked.

He shook his head and clenched his fists. "No, it all happened too quickly. I yelled at the nurse when she came to the bed and told her what happened. But she obviously didn't believe me, just told me I'd had a nightmare."

Mike and I looked at each other wondering what to make of it. I remembered what had happened to my car a few months before and the figure who'd been following me that night. It sort of lent credence to what Peter had just said.

"What bothers me," Pete went on, "is that this bloke will try to kill me again."

"I guess we have to presume that this is connected to Gajha. You're talking about a black man and all of this has happened since the conference that day in Hyde Park," I said.

"There's no doubt about that," Mike agreed. "There are too many vested interests involved. And they're obviously prepared to go all the way to stop us."

"So what do we do now?" I asked. "It seems to me we're in too deep to consider pulling out. And I, for one, don't want to do that. But we can't ignore all of this either. We've got to find some way of stopping these criminals."

"The problem is they're playing this game differently to us. They don't sit around and go over and over things like we do. They don't give a damn about anything other than protecting their own interests," Peter said. "And what's really got me worried is that they might try and hurt my family. I can't let that happen."

Mike nodded. "I know what you mean, mate. I'm in the same boat as you. My kids are at boarding school in Edinburgh at the moment, but when they come back here, that's another thing."

"What about putting this in the hands of the police?" I suggested. "We've got nothing to lose by doing that."

"Maybe but they'd probably think the same as the nurse did, given the circumstances," Peter said, emptying his glass. "We've got to keep our eyes and ears open and tell Claire and Sarah, and maybe even Gwyn, to not go walking in the street alone, or at least for the time being."

After a couple more drinks, I said my goodbyes and left the pub at eleven o'clock, walking back to my flat not too far from Sloane Square. It was another cold, wet night and the only sound I could hear in the street was the chattering of my teeth. I was used to the prosthesis now, which allowed me to walk at a reasonable pace through the fog, and I got home surprisingly quickly, only to find when I did, that the heavy iron door at the front of the building had been left ajar. I figured one of the tenants had forgotten to close it behind him, but when I went to close the door, I saw that the lock was jammed, and gave up after a couple of attempts to close it.

The lift was on one of the upper floors, so I waited for it to come down, looking at my watch, remembering that I hadn't left any food out for Morris. The poor old cat could hardly move because of arthritis in his hind legs, and depended on me totally.

I was thinking about that when I opened the door to my flat and turned on the light in the vestibule, only to see it go straight out again. "Damn! That's all I need." I cursed, leaving the door open to shed light inside, and seeing an envelope on the floor near the door. I picked it up and walked to my study where the wind was blowing through the window that to my surprise had been left open. "Morris, where are you?" I called out a couple of times as I turned the desk lamp on and saw a trail of pages thrown everywhere. And the photograph frame with Marie in it broken on the floor. I bent down, lifted it up, and picked the broken glass that covered her photo off.

After I cleaned the mess up and closed the window, I looked at the letter, and smiled when I realized that it was from Marie. I opened it and read its contents slowly.

She talked about the progress in the building of the new pavilion that would increase the size of the clinic and the space for the cages inside. She told me in detail about Nina getting bigger, about her personality that seemed to Marie more human than ape now. She'd become the spoiled girl of Gambala and was always looking for someone's arms to keep her protected in most of the day. She finished that part of the letter, by saying that she didn't see much of a future for her in the wild upon her release.

UMAG seemed to be getting weaker and was possibly on the verge of collapse, due to political pressure and a constant barrage of negative publicity on the radio. She praised our efforts and insisted that we continue on. If The United Friends of Tanzania had achieved as much as it had, in only a few months, then the prospects were good to get the environment back on its feet.

On a personal level she told me that she missed our moments together terribly, and was anxious to see me back at Gambala as soon as possible, and finished the letter by telling me she loved me.

I folded the letter, wishing I was with her right then, and that I could repeat those three simple words to her. How much did it count for, to hear the right woman say, I love you, and to say it back to her, feeling how true and deep the feeling was. It was what life was all about.

I stood up and started to look for Morris. "Come here, old fellow. Where are you? Come on, stop playing games, come out from wherever you are! Aren't you hungry, Morris?"

But despite my words and the fact that he always

appeared when I came home, this time he was nowhere to be seen. I looked underneath the furniture, in wardrobes, in the kitchen, and in his favourite hiding place of all, under my bed. But he wasn't anywhere. I started to get worried and wondered whether he'd climbed out the window and hadn't been able to find his way back.

I hurried back to the study and opened the window again and looked out, running my eye over the rusty emergency stairs that ran all the way up the building. "Morris, where are you?" But the only sound I heard was the sound of water coming from the stone fountain on the inner patio.

I slumped on the armchair inside, after several fruitless minutes of calling his name out. The whole thing seemed strange, sitting there, still holding the broken photo frame in my hands, feeling guilty that I hadn't left the food out for my cat.

I closed my eyes trying to work out what to do. I didn't know whether I should go out looking for him or wait where I was for his return. And in the middle of my confusion I put the television on, zapped through the channels with the remote control in my hand and finished up staring at the photo of Marie on my legs. She was the only thing that mattered now, I thought, running my finger over her beautiful face. After all those long months without her, I knew that well enough now.

I sat there for I don't know how long, with my eyes closed, going back over all my memories of being with Marie in Gambala, when suddenly I heard a creak in a wooden board in the corridor, and opening my eyes became aware straight away that someone was standing behind me.

CHAPTER
THIRTY-FOUR

I jumped out of the armchair and span around, ready for anything or anyone, but not for who was standing there before me.

"I'm sorry, John, I didn't mean to scare you," Jackie said, walking up to me and kissing me on the cheek.

"What are you doing here, Jackie? It's very late. How did you get in?"

"You left the door open. Just as well it was only me. I rang the bell, but it looks like it doesn't work."

I tried to calm down, pointing at the sofa. "Please, sit down, Jackie. I've never believed in miracles you know."

She looked at me strangely. "You mean, me coming here?"

"Yes," I said, sitting down beside her, noting her interest in Marie's photo that was still on top of the table.

She settled back on the sofa and said, "I wasn't sure whether to come here or not. But I have to admit that I haven't stopped thinking about your sudden appearance at the clinic the other day. I guess there are a few things that need clearing up."

"Thanks for coming, Jackie."

"I'm not doing it for you, John. It's only for Sophie," she pointed out. "I never thought I'd see you again. I came because I wanted to make it clear, that as far as Sophie's concerned, you are…"

"Dead?" I said, without thinking. "You told her I died?"

"No, John," she said shaking her head. "In spite of the fact that I loved and hated you like no one else in my life, I have to confess I didn't have the courage to even kill you with words. When she asked me who you were, I was tempted to tell her the truth. But I just told her, you were a good friend from my school days. She knows that her father is alive, but that he was too young to assume the responsibility for her when I fell pregnant. And that I decided to bring her up alone. I told her the truth in other words."

My eyes opened wider, and my jaw dropped further with each of her words.

"That's how it was, John. And that's how it is. She's got a very good father in Thierry, but she knew from the beginning that he wasn't her real father," she said, her chin trembling, tears welling up in her eyes.

"Then why didn't she say something when you mentioned my name at the clinic?"

"She only knows you as Jonathan. Perhaps she didn't make an association and I'm certainly not going to take it any further. I'm only here because I needed to clear that up with you. And to ask you for the love that we once shared to not approach Sophie. I've dedicated my whole life to making her happy, and the chance of your appearance creating an inner chaos in her, is a risk I'm not prepared to run. Do you understand?"

It was a long and poignant explanation and I could only nod in agreement. "Unfortunately, I understand you only too well. How could I just walk up to her now and tell her I'm her father, after not having been around all these years. Forgive me, Jackie. I was a complete good-for-nothing, a person who only thought of himself. But rest assured I've paid a price for all that. My life hasn't been easy, I can tell you. I finished up making the same mistake my father did. I should've known that somewhere down the line, the bill comes in."

I looked away from her and back through the window. It made sense not to rush what I was saying. "You've given me a lesson in how life should be lived, Jackie. I'm not ever going to forget that. I just hope you can find it in your heart to forgive me."

She answered that straight away. "I forgave you a long time ago, John. You gave me the best thing that's happened to me in my life. Every time she says, mummy, to me, I just feel sorry for you that you've never enjoyed the privilege of being the father of the most beautiful girl in the world."

Her words cut through me like a knife. I'd never felt so much pain in my life.

She reached out and took me softly by the wrist. "I forgive you, John. Now we are adults and responsible for our own lives. Let's leave the past that hurt us both so badly, behind. I hope you find happiness. I really do."

The more I listened to her enviable maturity, the more I realized how much I'd lost. I looked at the photo of Marie, which seemed to be listening in on the conversation. "Jackie, thanks so much for coming and telling me all of this. Everything you've said is completely right. But there's a long road ahead. Just give me the hope that maybe someday I could get to know Sophie just a little."

Her expression changed instantly. "I've already told you that…"

"Wait! Give me a chance to explain myself. I understand that you don't want me close to either you or Sophie. But I swear to you that all these years have been hell for me. Without knowing it, I always felt that I had a daughter. She's followed me around in my dreams all that time. Asking me why I left her. Not knowing her has worn me out over the years."

"I don't know what to say to you, John. You're asking me for something that I don't think I can ever give you."

"I understand. But think it over, please. Don't give me a flat 'no' right now. Maybe, you'll look at it differently later on. Things change, and maybe she will to. I could always just be your friend visiting, if you'd prefer it that way."

Jackie sighed, moved on the sofa. "Ok, I'll think about it, John. I can't give you an answer now. Let's just leave it at that."

"Take as much time as you want. But I know you, and I know you're not a woman to carry a grudge all your life. You've already shown me that. And even though our lives have taken different directions, I want you to know that you'll always have a special place in my heart. I'm happy that you found Thierry. And everything's worked out well for you," I said, deciding it was better to leave it there. Besides, there wasn't too much more I could say.

She stood up, picked her bag up and gave me a couple of soft pats on the shoulder. "Let's see what time tells us, John. Nothing's written in stone."

I watched her walk out of the room, wondering what the future held for both of us. "And I'll close the door behind me," she called out when she made it there.

"Ok, thanks," I called back, sitting like a statue on the sofa. I was glad she'd come, felt a stab of relief in the pit of my stomach. And after a long while going over the whole conversation in detail, I suddenly remembered Morris.

I decided to go out into the street and do a round of the blocks. And eventually walked into a park not that far from home. I imagined Morris hidden in some nook of a tree, waiting to be rescued by his master. I called his name over and over, until suddenly I heard the crunching of twigs not far from where I was. I stopped walking, and looked around, but could only see a dark shape disappear into the darkness of the bushes. I thought about the conversation with Peter at the pub, and decided after nearly an hour and a half of looking for Morris that it was time to go home. I only hoped that Morris had miraculously appeared in my absence, because as I walked back, I feared that he'd disappeared forever.

I threw myself into bed when I got back, my mind a whirlpool of thoughts. Jackie's visit rather than giving me the sense of relief that I'd imagined earlier, had now confused me more than ever. Such goodness and nobility couldn't be real. How could she just forgive and forget as easily as that? Or was it possible that I was comparing her way of thinking with my own? I still wasn't sure that I'd forgiven my father.

The mother of a friend told me years ago: "It's very hard to judge yourself, isn't it, John?" And her words came back to me as I began to see how different Jackie was from me. I suppose getting older, and having gone through everything that had happened to me, had given me the ability now, to step outside myself and really look at my own decisions dispassionately. And from what I could see from the ruffled sheets of my bed, Jackie was simply wiser than I was. And knew how to keep the door open on the future and work her way through the present, way better than I'd ever been able to do.

After a long night of taking myself to pieces, the morning light started filtering into the room, bringing with it a little serenity. And as I turned over, I suddenly realized that I had been lying in bed the whole night with my street clothes on.

I got up and looked at my watch. It was later than I'd thought, already past eleven and I should have been at *Geo World* twenty-five minutes before, for a meeting that had been set up with AGP (Anti Gold Predators), an association established with its prime focus centered on the defence and sovereignty of citizens affected in mining countries.

The intention of the meeting had been to develop a strategy to corner and publicly expose the management of Gajha and its henchmen. It was hoped that as a result of this strategy the Tanzanian Government, even though involved with the mine management, would be forced to impose new restrictions and controls over mine emissions.

I swung into action, stood up, took fresh clothes out of the closet and ran to the bathroom, putting my hand behind the shower curtain to turn the tap on. And while I was undressing, the phone rang several times before whoever was on the other end of the line, hung up. I didn't have any time to talk to anyone. I took my clothes off, threw them in the laundry basket and as I went to put a foot under the shower, suddenly, I stopped, as I felt a stabbing pain in my chest. I backed out, stumbled on the parapet, and fell backwards onto the floor, hitting the back of my head hard against the facing wall.

CHAPTER
THIRTY-FIVE

Still disorientated and dizzy from the knock on the head, I sat up, feeling a dull ache running through the back of my head. I put my hand on the back of my neck and discovered I was bleeding. I struggled up, and dragged myself to the edge of the bathtub, opening the shower curtain slowly again and looking in on the horrific scene that had caused my reaction. A dark shape was floating in an enormous pool of its own blood.

I turned the tap off shakily, watching the water disappear from under the dead and mutilated body of poor, old Morris. There was a knife sticking through a blood soaked note on his chest. The nausea that had caused me to fall before, came back again as I dragged myself over to the toilet and vomited my heart out, everything spinning around me. I stayed there on my knees, panting, trying to summon up the courage to look back at that grotesque scene.

Thoughts came storming back of those photos that

Peter had taken of Thabo, lying below on his death bed of rotting animal flesh. It had been that incident that had really initiated our response. And thinking that I found the courage to get off the floor and look for my camera. This wasn't going to go unpunished, and regardless of my feelings, photos were going to help.

I came back into the bathroom and, after taking innumerable shots, I stretched my hand out and took the knife out of his chest, extracting the note. I grabbed a towel and dried it as much as I could, and tried to decipher the message which consisted of a simple sentence: "If you don't stop the war now, the river of blood will keep flowing."

I screwed my face up in disgust, vividly aware of how far these people were prepared to go. Their reach extended a long way from Africa, and I had little doubt that whoever had written this note meant what he said.

I rolled Morris into a towel, said some consoling words to the bloody wrap in my hands, and felt a cold fury rising in the ensuing silence. I was angrier than I'd ever been in my life and wanted my pound of flesh back as soon as I could get it. I was never going to give up what we'd started. There was nothing more to lose. And as the note mentioned the word war, I was going to unleash a battle they'd never forget.

A few days after Morris's death and despite being aware of the sensationalism of the photos I'd taken of him, I decided to bring everyone in on what had happened, with the purpose of attacking Gajha, relentlessly and without mercy. But there was nothing to go on. No way of using the incident to our advantage.

CHAPTER
THIRTY-SIX

Almost three weeks later, after Morris's death, and after having travelled to Germany with Pete and Mike to inaugurate the First Summit of Environment and Human Rights of the village populations near African mines, we received a call from the office of *Geo World*, on our return to come to a meeting that afternoon.

A few minutes before four o'clock, the three of us were in a room adjoining the meeting room wondering what the urgency was all about. And a few minutes later Charles appeared through a glass door, with a dark expression on his face and invited us into the meeting room where five others were seated around the oval table.

"Take a seat," he said, pointing to the three empty chairs remaining. "We called you here today because we received some news this morning that I'm afraid could have an important bearing on the future of our cause."

The three of us looked at each other, uncertain of

what to make of what he'd just said, or his apparently serious tone of voice.

"What's going on, Charles?" Peter asked.

"Things have turned for the worse," he said, stone-faced.

"Get to the point, Charles. You've got us dangling by a thread here," I said.

Then, to confuse us even more, Charles face broke out in a smile. "Gajha's dead!"

"What are you talking about?" The three of us almost said in unison.

Then all the others around the table got up and started clapping.

"What the hell's going on?" Mike asked looking around him.

"We've won the war, my friends," Charles said, raising his fist. "After almost three months of waiting, Interpol has given us the information we needed about McMahon and Dormonth."

"And what have they found out?" Pete asked, his hands under his chin.

"They've both got a darker past than you could have imagined," Charles explained. "It works out that McMahon was American before he was English."

"American?" I inquired, remembering McMahon's posh English accent.

"That's right. Let me give you some more details. McMahon fought in the Vietnam War in the sixties. But he apparently deserted in the middle of a battle, and later made his way to England where he asked for political asylum. A few years after that, he got his residency papers."

"Unbelievable," I said. "I couldn't pick his accent."

"He's clever," Mike said. "He must be, to have got where he is now."

"Wait, there's more to come," Charles said, lifting a folder in the air. "A few months after moving into a flat in London, he started rubbing shoulders with high society and finished up marrying Penelope Radcliffe, the daughter of Sir William Radcliffe, a prominent businessman and major shareholder of the Marren Gold Mine in Ghana. Through the support and contacts of his millionaire father-in-law, he gradually introduced himself into the gold industry.

"That's disgusting!" Peter said. "A traitor and a bloody liar. One can only imagine what he did with all that power."

"Exactly. But what about Dormonth and Phillipe the Belgian? Did they find something? " I asked, intrigued.

"Indeed. However, both have completely different reports," Charles said, beginning to read from the report. "It mentions here that Dormonth was abandoned as a child by his parents in an orphanage in Dublin and was subsequently adopted by an Irish family at the age of seven. His foster father had an administrative job in a Scottish coal mine. According to this, he was known for being extremely ambitious and ruthless with people beneath him, always trying to get himself into positions of power. By the time he was twenty-eight, he was involved in gold smuggling and arms trafficking. That was how he got himself ensconced in the world of gold mining, providing armament support to these countries and bribing officials with the weapons he had access to. It says in this blue folder here, that Dormonth is the main culprit when it comes to arms trafficking, and McMahon, on the other hand, is responsible for most human abuses and violations and is more involved in the dirty mining business. Intimidation and corruption are the norm, and there's hardly any investment in basic equipment because of McMahon. However, it goes without saying that both of them have been siphoning off vast wads of cash from both businesses."

"What else does the report say?" Mike asked.

"Phillipe Deneuve, it says, comes from a middle class Belgian family, and that he spent almost all his life in a coastal town called De Haan, close to Brujas. He studied at the University of Ghent in Belgium. Besides being a renowned veterinary doctor and specialist in infectious diseases, he lives in Brussels with his wife and two children, one a twenty-three-year-old and the other eighteen. He offers his services to several natural reserves in Africa, Gambala included. There doesn't appear to be anything shady in his past."

Despite Charles asseverations, I had my doubts about the lack of proof against Phillipe. I was convinced that there was a lot to find out about him beneath the façade of respectability that he apparently maintained. I was going to keep after him on my own account.

"The best news of all of this and the reason we called you here today," Charles said, smiling, "is that five days ago, to be precise, Cofy Mangandi bowed to international pressure and closed Gajha. After all this mess about McMahon and Dormonth came out, he's temporarily withdrawn the mine's operating license. As well as facing up to a vast amount of proof that there are anomalies in the accounts, the contracts, the acquisitions and the corresponding permits. No tax has been paid to the Tanzanian government in the last few years. A Supreme Court petition is already under way against Gajha and other mines in the region. But Gajha is the first that's received a closure order upon it. After all of this, when it does reopen, it will be under strict environmental supervision and subject to regular international inspections."

We were all impressed. It had been a wonderful morning. "And where are McMahon and Dormonth now?" I asked.

"They've been relieved of their positions," Charles explained. "And an impressive cache of weapons has been found at Gajha, and investigations are continuing."

"Well, after all of this, they can't stay out of jail much longer," Peter suggested.

"I suppose that will be the case," Charles agreed. "Cofy Mangandi's got to come out of this squeaky clean. And the only way he can do that, is to make an example of these two Englishmen and wipe his hands of the whole affair. His political nous might just let him finish, being painted a national hero after all this is over!"

"And his nephew Kassim Mangandi? What's happened to him?" I asked.

"Reading between the lines," Charles said. "I think they're going to throw the bucket over the others. I mean, we're talking Africa here. Anything you can accuse the colonial powers of, goes down very well these days there. Blame the whole lot on greedy and manipulative Englishmen sounds like the way out to me."

Mike was nodding in agreement. "Yes, they got in first before their own heads were on the chopping block. They probably reasoned that they didn't have any choice."

Ian, from Amnesty International, had been listening to the proceedings without saying a word, but he ventured an opinion now. "What worries me is the impact that this is going to have on the thousands of workers left without a job. Desperate and hungry people are capable of doing anything."

"No one still knows what will come out of all of

this. But it's without doubt the best news I've had in a long time," Peter said, rubbing his hands in glee.

Mike wasn't left short either. "Thanks a heap, *Geo World*, none of this would've been possible without your help."

As soon as the meeting was over, I sent Marie a telegram advising her of what had happened, and telling her also that the three of us would be coming back to Gambala in the next few weeks to celebrate our victory, personally with her. I asked her to pass the news on to Mummbar and Turner, and tell them that we'd bring a bottle of the best champagne with us, which we'd uncork upon our arrival.

Pete and Mike came to my flat later that night to go over our plans for the trip, while we toasted the sweet success that seemed to have just fallen out of the sky.

"And what's your next step with Marie?" Mike asked lighting a cigarette, as he leaned back on the sofa. "Are you going to give everything up, like you said you would, and go and live in the jungle with the apes? With the mud and dust, and without a pub around for thousands of miles, or even a bloody telephone to ring your dear friends here?"

"That sounds like a terrible sacrifice," Peter laughed, raising his glass at the same time. "But I think Marie's worth it, don't you?"

"Besides, no one would put up with John, other than Marie," Mike joked. "She's a strong and passionate woman, with a lot of guts and as domineering as all hell!"

The laughter continued before Pete suggested: "And that's what you always needed, my dear friend. Forgive me for saying it, but your personal life has never lived up to its potential. Now's the hour to correct that, don't you think?"

"I know, Pete. I have to admit that no one has ever

made me feel the way I do with her, " I said in a serious tone that cut through their joking. "I love her and I'll let you in on a secret. I'm going to ask her to marry me."

"Bravo!" Mike exclaimed as Pete raised his eyebrows in surprise.

"Are you serious, John?" Pete asked, incredulously.

"Just as you heard it, my friends. I'm a changed man. During the last few months here, I've appreciated all the more, the time I spent with her on the reserve. I've missed the simplicity, the beauty and the naturalness of life there. I'm not going to let this opportunity pass to live with the woman I love."

"You surprise me when I hear you talking like that," Mike said. "You are indeed a changed man. I congratulate you, mate. It's been a day of great news."

"No doubt," Pete said, raising his glass. "John will come to his senses one day."

It was obvious that neither of them really believed that I could take this step after years of emotional instability. But it seemed the most natural thing in the world for me to do now. Marie was in my thoughts all day long. I couldn't imagine a life without her.

But Mike was still in a mood for jokes. "Pete, can you imagine the family that John and Marie are likely to have? Babies and baboons walking around hand in hand. And talking about that, whatever happened to little Nina?"

"Marie says she's very well and that she's a leader of sorts to the younger ones."

"Well, I'll be," Mike said, extending his hand to shake mine. "She sounds just like her parents, mate."

It was a night to laugh, to let our hair down, after many hard months of working and worrying where we were going. Everything seemed so much easier after the good news.

CHAPTER
THIRTY-SEVEN

A week after the news I read an article about the disintegration of UMAG, in which it made mention of the complete disagreement among party members and mining sympathizers, who'd counter attacked President Mangandi and his gang of corrupt politicians. They revealed the abuses and constant mishandling they had endured during his government and argued that due to threats received over the years, they had had to act in their own self defence, violating at the same time the rights that they had been denied arbitrarily.

In the meantime, they expressed their repulsion for the unscrupulous behaviour of the president who had been, according to them, involved in the scandal from the very beginning and was now just trying to wash his hands of the whole affair.

A Pandora's Box had been opened, releasing the anger and resentment of all those involved. And the government's opponents were working tirelessly to reinstate new management and to recover the workers' jobs. They'd lost income and had slowly become birds of prey, looking to pick their way through whatever got in their way.

I was amazed to see the reach and impact that power and money had on the principles and values that people had: one day they were brothers and friends, and the next, sworn enemies fighting to the death.

I confirmed in the weeks that followed that more wealth implies less loyalty. People were climbing over each other's bodies, trying to get to the podium of power and become the owners of the gold.

One morning while I was picking through the heap, trying to work out who was good and who was bad, the phone rang. I picked it up. "John?" a hoarse voice asked on the other end of the line.

"Yes, who's that?"

A smile crossed my face when I heard his answer. "Mummbar. How are you, John?"

"How good is it to hear your voice, man," I told him. "Did you get the good news?"

"Yes, that's why I'm ringing. Bill Turner's standing next to me, I'll put him on."

A second later I heard Turner's unmistakable voice. "John..."

"Bill, it's great you rang. You've called at just the right time. Everything's worked out just as we'd hoped. They're all fighting each other, now that Gajha's collapsed. You've got no idea how happy that's made me feel. I guess you're feeling the same there, aren't you?"

"That's why we're ringing. We want the three of you to come to Gambala, as soon as you can."

"No problem. We're planning on coming in two weeks. I'll bring a case of champagne. How's that sound? I'm dying to get back there."

"I can imagine but..., could you bring the trip forward to this weekend? It'd be good if you could."

"Has something happened?" I asked, as I felt the call change direction. "What's the urgency?"

"Calm down, John. Just book the first plane you can, and leave the details at my office in Shinyanga, so that Samson can be waiting for you."

I began to form a dozen questions in my head, all of which hadn't been answered yet. "But Bill?"

"I've got to hang up, John. I can hardly hear you. There's a lot of interference. It's better to see you in the flesh," he said without any further explanation.

I rested the receiver on my shoulder, going over the conversation that had just finished. I lay back down on the bed and heaped both pillows behind my back, but after only a few seconds lying there, I jumped out of bed, threw my clothes on and headed straight for the travel agency at Victoria Station, where I bought a ticket on the first available flight out. Turner's insistence alarmed me. But I figured in the end that they were just impatient to share the good news with me. Besides, what was the point in waiting another two weeks; the sooner the better.

After Victoria Station, I went to *Geo World* to go over a few outstanding points with Charles and then made a short stop at Singh Jewellers, with the idea of buying an engagement ring for Marie. But sitting in front of tray after a tray of different rings, I started to feel a range of emotions that I could never have imagined before. I should've been overwhelmed by the staggering display of classic and exotic rings, full of precious stones in every conceivable setting. But I wasn't, I was enthralled instead, carefully studying each and every one.

In the end, I chose a delicate sapphire mounted in a simple ring of white gold. It reminded me of my grandmother's wedding ring, which gave it added significance. If I could build a relationship as strong and intense as the one Manny had with my grandfather, then my future together with Marie was going to be one of the great wonders of the world.

CHAPTER
THIRTY-EIGHT

After arranging a few final details, I packed my bag that afternoon, putting as many books as I could pack in, as well as my music recorder, a hat, my camera, the bottle of champagne we would drink the toast with when I got to Gambala, and of course the most important thing of all: Marie's engagement ring.

I called Gwyn who'd moved a few months before to Manchester, and advised her that I didn't think I'd be back in London for a few months. She wished me luck, told me once more how sorry she was about Morris, and let me know that the only thing that was important to her was my happiness.

"Thanks, Gwyn. You've always been there for me over the years," I told her, meaning every word I said, before hanging up.

There was a thunderstorm outside as I made it to the street and hailed a taxi which took me to Piccadilly Station. I took the tube to Heathrow from there and around an hour later than I'd planned, joined the queue to the counter at the airport.

I was very late, and glanced at my watch constantly, but was able to jump the queue a little later when an announcement came over the intercom for a few stragglers, myself included, to make their way directly to the counter, and from there I got a saloon passage through customs to the boarding gate.

I was standing there along with the other passengers waiting to board the aircraft, when I suddenly realized that I didn't have my boarding pass in hand. I looked through my hand luggage, my pockets, around me on the floor, but found nothing. It wasn't the sort of pressure I needed right then so I bolted back along the corridor, looking everywhere, until I got back to the boarding area entry point. I had no idea where I'd lost the pass, couldn't find it anywhere and grumpily trudged back to the boarding gate and told one of the stewardesses, standing at the counter, what had happened.

"John Carmichael, you say? Yes, here it is. You must have dropped it on the floor, and somebody was kind enough to pick it up and hand it in. Can I see your passport please?"

I gave it to them, and a few minutes later, I was adjusting my seat belt on board the plane, smiling for the first time in a few hours, watching London disappear through a shuddering window, as we took off.

After making a long stopover at Jomo Kenyatta Airport in Nairobi, the long, thirteen-hour flight came to an end and I was back in the capital of Tanzania, back in the chaos, fighting my way for an hour through baggage collection, and the teeming airport population, to Samson, casually reading a newspaper in the waiting van outside.

"How are you doing, Samson?" I asked walking up to the door.

"Mister John!" he said, folding the paper quickly and getting out to help me. "You look tired, Mister John. How was the trip?"

"Long, my friend, very long. No other way to describe it. How are things going with you?" I asked him after he'd accommodated the bags in the boot, and we'd both got into the car.

"Things haven't been good around here since the news."

"What news are you talking about?" I asked him.

"All this about the president and the mine," he said, checking his next comment as if he was going to regret saying too much. "Mister Turner and Mummbar will tell you all that, though. The plane is waiting to take you to Shinyanga. And the leg? It looks like you've got a new one."

I laughed, stretching the prosthesis out in front of me. "That's right, Samson. There are moments when I forget that it isn't really a part of me. I've got so used to it now."

"Life's strange," he said, looking at my legs. "But it's good to see you walking without those crutches."

"You're not wrong there, Samson."

"I think you and I are made of the same stuff, Mister John. We never give up," he mentioned, smiling, as we drove on through the chaotic traffic to the smaller airport, where a plane was waiting. "May God be with you, Mister John. He lights the way. Don't lose faith," Samson said, after putting my bags on the plane, and watching me get on board.

I was surprised by the sincerity of his words and didn't know what to say. "Thank you, Samson," I said as I discovered that all the other seats on the plane were empty. I was the only passenger on board, and as the plane roared down the tarmac, all the old feelings of insecurity came storming back. I opted to listen to music instead of my fears, and took my recorder out of the briefcase and put my headphones on, and went in a different direction in my head with my eyes closed, as the plane took off over the savanna.

A few minutes later, and thinking of Marie, I took the jewellers case out of the briefcase and lifted the ring up, looking at the myriad shades of blue that seemed to explode out of the delicate sapphire. I put it back into the box and then into my coat pocket and closed my eyes again, thinking of seeing Marie in a few hours, and the expression on her face when I gave her the ring.

Minutes later I heard the pilot's voice saying, "I'm sorry, sir. But we won't be able to land at Shinyanga, because of bad weather. We'll land at a town near Gambala instead."

I sat up straight and looked through the window at the pelt of rain outside, and a short while later, we landed at a small airfield that was already half covered by water. But then, there was a van there near the tarmac, but no driver, and instead of waiting for one to appear, and after getting some instructions from the pilot, I drove off before the whole airfield was under water. The road I took was forming itself into a great quagmire, and I hadn't got too far before a great curtain of water cut visibility to almost zero. I was getting nervous, and could see myself getting stuck at any moment, still a long way from Gambala. But then, almost miraculously, the clouds lifted to reveal the most beautiful rainbow I'd ever seen stretching across the vastness of the savanna. I looked in the rear vision mirror to see the storm disappearing behind me and smiling, looked back at the road ahead to see a person waving their hand in the distance. And as I got closer, my heart took a sudden leap when I realized it was Marie. I pushed the accelerator to the board, speeding through fresh mud, towards her, and to my amazement, Nina was in her arms.

The first kiss was deep and carried with it the weight of our months apart, and when I took my lips from hers, I kissed her eyelids, her cheeks and her neck. I couldn't get enough of her, or she of me, while Nina complained about that, looking up from the ground below where she'd been left. We picked her up and walked under the cover of a large acacia tree and looked at the glow of Urekewe in the distance, under the warm blanket of sunset.

"I've missed you so much, John. I've been waiting so long for this day to tell you I love you."

I ran my mouth across her cheek, smelt the perfume of her skin that I'd carried all this time in my memory, and felt the beating of my heart accelerate, when suddenly, in a blinding flash, her face began to fade away from my hands.

CHAPTER
THIRTY-NINE

Stressed and breathing heavily, I looked up, and discovered to my profound regret, that it had all been a mirage. I looked through the window and realized that we'd already landed at Shinyanga Airport. I sighed, trying to twist out of that sweet dream, as the pilot, the same one who'd flown me to Dar es Salaam the last time, opened the side door.

"It was good that you were able to sleep during the flight," he said. "I didn't get a chance to talk to you up there, but it's good to see you again."

"Thanks," I said, shaking his hand, and noting Bantu in the distance, standing next to the truck.

"Welcome back, John," he called out to me as I walked towards him.

"It's great to see you, Bantu. What's news?"

"Not much, John," he said, throwing my bag into the back seat, before making his way around to the other side. "Not much at all."

We drove off with the radio on, and Bantu singing in Swahili, but a kilometre from Gambala, he turned the radio off, sighed, and studied both sides of the road carefully. Both he and Samson had one thing in common, they could both move from euphoria to the other extreme in less than a second.

He seemed nervous, scratching his chin, looking around, and when we arrived at the main entrance, I saw that the gate had been smashed to pieces. "What happened here, Bantu?" He didn't answer, just shrugged his shoulders, while we continued on in complete silence. The further we went the more worried I became, as I could see the pavilions ahead in ruins, covered in ash. Almost half of the external cages were destroyed and empty, as we drove by to one wing of the main pavilion that was still standing. "What happened here, Bantu? Tell me now!"

But before he could say anything, Turner and Mummbar appeared in the distance. They both looked grim. I got out of the truck and walked up to them. "Tell me what happened here, Bill?"

He put his hand on my arm without saying anything and looking over his shoulder, I saw Phillipe standing on a landing of the stairs, holding a paintbrush in his hand. My blood was boiling and I walked past the others straight for him, grabbing him by the shirt collar, pushing him back, my eyes pressed into his, yelling, telling him what a low life traitor he was. I figured he was behind the fire that had raged through the Reserve, and on the point of landing my first punch into his miserable head, Turner grabbed me from behind. "Wait, John! What are you doing?" he demanded to know.

I struggled to free myself and let my rage flow out, but Turner said firmly, "Enough, John. I didn't want you to come here to do this. Calm down, mate."

"He's a piece of garbage who's tricked everyone," I said, still furious. "He's in cahoots with UMAG and I'm sure he was with McMahon that day at the mine. Deny it if you can!" I challenged him, looking him straight in the eye.

"It's not what you think, John," Phillipe tried to explain.

"It's my turn to talk," Turner said, interrupting him, and grabbing me by the arm. "We already know all about this. I'll explain it all now. Let's go for a walk." Stunned by what Turner had just said, I followed him away from the building, while the other two, standing as still as two statues, stayed where they were.

We stopped at some wooden bench seats carved out of tree trunks, where we could see the hollow clearly, a few pieces of my dream coming back to me, as Turner asked me to take a seat.

"I can tell you, you're way off the mark as far as Phillipe's concerned," he said, after a long silence. "He told us about all of this some time ago. It was the only way he could find out about the miners' plans and the only way they'd trust him with their secrets. I can tell you, that thanks to Phillipe, quite a few leaders of UMAG have fallen into the trap. It was all Phillipe's idea, and he kept it from us until he knew that he had a chance to bring them down. I'm sorry that we couldn't tell you earlier. But as you can see..." he said looking at the remains of the pavilions. "Not everything worked out as we'd planned. Fortunately, most of UMAG'S leaders are in jail. And McMahon and Dormonth are nearly ready to join them. I can tell you now, John, that Galijha didn't die as we thought he had."

"What? What are you saying? Galijha died in the mine with Thabo. I saw that with my own eyes."

"Well, he made a remarkable recovery," Turner said sarcastically. "It seems like that night in Sector 38 was exactly what he wanted us to think."

"And what has all that got to do with all this then?" I asked, looking at the devastation around me.

"Two days after finding out the news about the situation at Gajha, the imprisonment of its leaders that I mentioned, and after thousands of workers lost their jobs, the war really started around here. It became public knowledge that we had a prime role in bringing the mine down. We found out that Galijha had been coerced into siding with them against his will. They threatened his family. In actual fact they killed his youngest son. Only a few days ago, we discovered that they'd sent one of their accomplices to London."

The whole story was becoming clearer. "Now I understand everything."

"How do you mean, John?"

"This man that you're talking about sounds like the one that stole some papers from my car, tried to kill Peter at the clinic and also killed my cat."

"I'm sorry to hear that," Turner said. "I'm sorry that you got into this whole sorry affair in the first place. If I had known what was going to happen, I would never have got you involved."

I could feel his thoughts running over the memory of his dead son, Roger.

"I understand what you're saying," I told him. "But I can tell you that if I get hold of that criminal, I'm going to skin him alive with my own bare hands."

"I think he's already under arrest," Turner informed me. "But getting back to what I was telling you before, it was Phillipe who trapped Galijha the day of the fire."

"Phillipe trapped him?" I asked, incredulously.

"As far as we could find out, Galijha had his hands

tied and was forced to perpetrate one crime after the next with the group from UMAG that eventually attacked the Reserve."

"Galijha did all of that? I can't believe it. I thought he was against any form of violence."

Turner shook his head. "Not really, it was him all along, with the other workers from the mine, who started the fire that destroyed most of the Reserve. It was early one morning and they took us all by surprise. They destroyed almost all the cages. Some animals escaped, but luckily thanks to Phillipe, we could put the fire out before it burned everything down. We were able to rescue several animals and workers who were trapped." A film of cold sweat began forming on my forehead as I listened to him, as I sensed there was still more to come.

"They set fire to the first pavilions, and Phillipe, who was the first to realize what was going on, activated the alarm. But it was too late for some. The fire was already raging through the rooms."

The sweat was flowing freely now, a lump had formed in my throat. "Where's Marie? And Nina?"

Turner grimaced, bit his lip and looked away from me. "Nina suffered burns but fortunately she's recovering well now, and Marie, well, Phillipe got her out still alive, but…"

CHAPTER
FORTY

It was like I'd been shot through the heart, and lying wounded, was waiting for the final brutal words to come. "Marie died three days after the fire."

I began to cry like I'd never cried in my life, the news of her death ripping what peace and happiness there was in my soul from their very foundations. I was already a skeleton walking, only minutes after hearing Marie's fate. My life had become a living nightmare.

"For God's sake, why didn't you tell me?" I said spitting the words out like bullets. "My place was here at her side."

"She didn't want you to see her that way, John. She wanted you to remember her as she was. Besides…" he said, handing me a tape recorder. "She knew you would come, and she recorded this for you before she died."

Without knowing where we were going, we walked in silence until we came to a beautiful clearing that was tinged pink and gold in the sunset, just as it had been in my dream. We stopped in front of a mound of earth, into which a wooden cross with a crown of green leaves was planted. The plaque read: Marie Louise Dubois 1966-1995, and under her name, Loved by Africa.

Crying, I fell to my knees in front of her grave, as Turner left me alone. The sky had turned red, spreading its glow across the vastness of the savanna, as a few light drops of rain wept upon the earth. I was in the most beautiful place, in the saddest moment of my life. I stood up, and sat down on a rock beside the grave, and placing the recorder on my knees, I pressed the play button and the Beatles' song "Yesterday" started up, interrupted by Marie's weak and fragile voice. "Johnny, when you hear my voice, you know that my heart is with you. Close your eyes and let me stay at your side." I followed her advice, struggling to imagine her beside me. "Time allowed us to be together, and gave me the opportunity to discover that there is something between us that will last forever. Life isn't what we see, but what we will feel and have felt. And despite the distance, Johnny, I will carry you with me wherever I go."

There was a pause on the tape, and I begged her to go on. "Please, Marie, don't stop now."

"Johnny, I'm carrying your voice, your smile, your kisses and your touch with me. I will remember you every night of eternity. Death is only an illusion. A painful void, but our soul and essence live on forever. Smile my beloved."

I tried to do as she had said, but sighed weakly instead.

"Don't waste these precious moments on being sad. We will always be together in spirit. Be happy, Johnny," she said as her voice faded to a murmur. "There is a reason for everything. Hold me in your heart. I love you, Johnny, and I always will."

The sadness was overwhelming. I took the small grey jeweller's box out of my pocket, took the ring out, and after placing it on top of the mound, pushed it into the earth. The sun was sinking fast now, and with my eyes closed, I imagined Marie in my arms. But my love for her was much bigger than my heart could bear. I gave it to her with my hands, as she came into my body, where she would sleep for the rest of my life.

During the four months that followed, I stayed on at Gambala, helping Nina to recover and lending a hand in the rebuilding of the Reserve. Peter and Mike arrived three weeks after that mournful day, and helped me slowly to get over her death. I couldn't leave Gambala that easily; leave the place that had meant so much to Marie. I had to see it strong again first, with its mission to preserve life, rediscovered. But one morning, around Easter, when the savanna rains came, I knew that the time had come to close that chapter on my life and move forward. It was time to go home.

The publishing house,
CBH Books,
a division of Cambridge BrickHouse, Inc.,
was created to encourage excellence in literature.
We publish works in all genres, in all languages,
in the U.S. and abroad.
For more information on how to publish with CBH
Books,
please visit our website:
www.cbhbooks.com